JF
WAT

 W9-CEU-737

JUN 1 4 2010

For Rebeccah and Hannah

ACKNOWLEDGMENTS

Thanks to Jim Watts and Deborah Hodge
for assistance with research.
My continuing gratitude to Sue Tate,
who helps make my every manuscript better than I
ever imagined it could be!

"I thought her unsinkable...I do not understand it."
          – Philip Franklin, vice president of the
          White Star Line, Monday, April 15, 1912.

London, England

1902

I

Johnny

The night before the picnic, Kathleen and I stayed awake long after Johnny had been brought to his room and settled in his crib. Unlike us, he'd been fast asleep for hours. Our Sunday dresses and aprons were draped over the back of the chair, the collars starched stiffly.

Kathleen and I had run over to the bedroom window half a dozen times to make sure it wasn't raining.

"Is it night yet?" I asked my big sister. "Where's the moon and the stars? When will it be time to go, Kath?"

"Will you hush, Lou? Mother's coming upstairs."

The door opened.

"One more word from either of you and you won't be going anywhere! Into bed with you, and stay there, before you wake up your little brother. Father says we're to leave by five," Mother said.

I jumped onto the bed, crawled over Kathleen, and burrowed under the thin blanket to my place near the wall. I squeezed my eyes shut so tightly that I could see colored spots beneath my eyelids.

"I'm sleeping," I said.

Close beside me, Kathleen shook with laughter before pushing the blanket away. "I'm so hot, Mother, I can't breathe," she said.

"What did I just say? I'm warning you, one more word and I'm going to tell Father."

We lay still, not daring to move until after we'd heard her go downstairs, into the kitchen, and close the door.

"Night, night, sleep tight, don't let the bedbugs bite," Kathleen said, and gave me a friendly pinch.

Neither of us had ever been on a train, let alone to the seaside. Mr. Dawson, the greengrocer for whom Father worked, had announced the firm's annual family outing was to Southend on Sea. This year, Mother said all three of us were old enough to go!

In the morning, I'd been too excited to eat breakfast. The swaying of the train made me feel sick. Getting off, I tripped down the steps. Johnny cried–he'd got soot in his eye. After Mother had taken the smut out with the corner of her handkerchief, Father hoisted

Johnny onto his shoulders. We followed him out of the station.

And there was the sea at last, waiting for us. It shone brighter than the scullery window Kathleen and I rubbed clean with newspaper and vinegar, every Saturday.

A hurdy-gurdy man played a barrel organ; his monkey wore a red waistcoat and danced on a chain. The man sang, and the tune made Kathleen and me skip along and Johnny clap his hands. Father said the man was from Italy. I asked if we were going there on the train, and Mother laughed. She forgot to tell us to walk nicely!

Behind us, the hurdy-gurdy man trundled the organ down the lane, wheels rattling over the cobbles. Past the stands selling eels and cockles and mussels, we all went. A few of the men threw coins into the monkey's little cap.

All along, as far as I could see, was water. I remember thinking it was more water than I'd ever seen before in my whole life! Father bought us a bottle of lemonade to share and promised us a walk on the pier, later in the day.

Kathleen asked, "Does the sea stretch all the way to Australia, Father?"

He winked at Mother and said, "Almost," and I knew it was a fib. But I didn't know where Australia was, so I never said anything.

We walked down some rocky steps onto the sand. Father paid the man for two deck chairs.

Mother said, "Jack, you don't need to do that–I brought a blanket to sit on."

Father said, "Nothing's too good for my Flo." He calls Mother Flo when he's in a good mood and Florence when he's had a bad day, but that's not often.

"Don't be daft," she said, smiling at him.

It was a happy day, and after we'd eaten our sandwiches, Mother shook the crumbs off the blanket for the gulls. She told us we could go and play. "Mind you don't go out of sight, and mind you watch your brother," she said, taking out her knitting. She always keeps busy doing something, but Father put his newspaper over his face and went to sleep. We turned round to wave to her, and she waved back.

Kathleen and I each held one of Johnny's hands. She carried the bucket and I carried the spade, and we ran with him down towards the water. Above us, the gulls screeched and swooped as they flew. I felt dizzy from the sound, from the taste of salt, from the smells of the day, and the warmth of the sun. I never wanted this lovely time to end.

We took off our boots and stockings and helped Johnny off with his. Kathleen lined the boots up in a tidy row beside a small rock. We grabbed Johnny's hands and jumped him over the rocks and pebbles, closer and closer to the waves that looked like the foam on Father's pint of beer.

"How old are you, Johnny? Say one, two," Kathleen said.

"One, two," he repeated after her.

We sat him down, and he stuck his fingers into the wet sand over and over and held them up to show us the grains of sand stuck to them. I dug a hole for him before Kathleen and I went looking for shells. I wanted pink ones to decorate the castle I was planning to build. For a while I heard Johnny humming to himself, happy as can be.

The sun shone hot on the back of my neck. The sky got bluer, and a breeze lifted my hair. Waves, aglitter with color, teased my toes, splashing my legs. I pulled my dress higher, hoping Mother couldn't see me. Filling my apron with shells, I brought them back to shore and began to make a pretty pattern.

"Wicked, wicked, girl!"

I looked up and there was Mother, shaking Kathleen. I was afraid I'd be in trouble too. *Had she seen me with my dress up?* I tried to brush the sandy streaks from my apron. Then I grabbed my boots and stockings and put them on as fast as I could. Johnny's were still there, but I couldn't see him. *Where was he? Had Father taken him on the pier without us?*

Then I heard two slaps—one, two—sharp, like wind slapping at sheets on wash day. Turning around, I saw Kathleen standing there, silent, her cheeks red. I ran over and took hold of her hand. I was five and she was seven, and we looked after each other.

"What have you done, Kathleen and Louisa Gardener? Look at your dirty frocks. I can't trust you for a minute! Didn't I tell you to watch your little brother? Answer me!" I closed my eyes, shutting out the glare of the sun and my mother's face. Her fingers dug into my shoulder.

"Look at me when I'm speaking to you." The voice didn't sound like Mother's.

Mrs. Bernardi came over. She put her arms around Mother and tried to pull her away. Father helped her, all the while talking quietly to Mother.

I heard him say, "Let the girls be, Flo, it won't bring him back." He picked up Johnny's boots, and we followed them, hearing the murmurs of the women gathered round us.

"Drowned, poor little mite. His father found him, lying face-down in the water."

"Who drowned, Kath?" I asked.

We'd left the bucket behind, and when I turned to look, I saw my spade sticking up in the water. The tide had already washed my shell pattern away.

"Shall I run back and fetch the bucket and spade? Will we get in trouble for leaving them, Kath?"

"Hush, Lou, never mind them. Johnny's drowned."

A small crowd had gathered, and a policeman was holding something wrapped in a blanket. A bare foot dangled against his uniform. A woman picked up Mother's knitting and put it in the hamper. It was late, too late to go on the pier, like Father had promised us.

Someone brought Mother a mug of tea. She took a sip and put the mug down on the sand.

A long, long time later, when we made our way slowly to the train station, the hurdy-gurdy man was still there, playing his tune. The policeman told him to move along. When I look back on that day, I always think he was playing for my brother.

It was dark by the time we got home.

"Where's the moon, Kath?" I asked.

"The moon is asleep," my sister said.

"Is Johnny asleep, Kath?"

"Yes."

After the funeral, after friends and neighbors had left, Mother came up to our room. Kathleen and I had been sitting on the edge of our bed for a long while. It was too hot to hold hands.

Mother's face looked hot too, red and blotchy, as if she'd been crying. "Come here," she said. We didn't move. She knelt down in front of us. "Johnny's never coming back," she said. "It shouldn't have happened, but it wasn't your fault. It was an accident, remember that." She got up and sat down on the bed between us. For a while, no one spoke. Mother reached out and clasped our hands in hers.

"We're sorry, Mother," Kathleen said.

"Sorry, I'll never do it again," I whispered, remembering my dirt-streaked Sunday frock and apron that Mother had to wash again before Johnny's funeral.

"We won't talk about Johnny anymore, just now. We'll go downstairs in a minute, and Father will give you a cuddle. I'll make something nice for your tea," Mother said.

"Will Johnny be there?" I asked.

"Hush, Lou," Kathleen said.

I put my head on Mother's lap, and Kathleen leaned against her arm.

Mother's voice was quiet—it sounded as if she were speaking from a long way off. "Our Johnny can't come back. He's gone to heaven to live with the angels. He's safe there."

Then, holding hands, we went downstairs, and I walked on tiptoes so as not to wake Johnny up.

Later, after we'd put ourselves to bed, after Mother had come in to say good night and we'd fallen asleep, something woke me. I sat up, looking at the moonlight shine through the window onto the bedroom floor, making it glisten like a pool of water. Like the sea where Johnny drowned.

Kathleen sat up beside me, rigid, hearing the sounds coming through the wall. We looked at each other.

"Is it a ghost, Kath?" I asked her. "Is it Johnny gone back to his room, crying for us?"

"Ghosts don't cry, silly. I'll go and see. Are you coming?" Kathleen slid out of bed.

I was afraid to be left alone, so I followed. Stepping fearfully across the pool of light on the floor that looked like water, I crept out. We listened at the door of Johnny's room.

"It's not a ghost at all," Kathleen said. And then, "Quick, get back to bed before Father finds us!"

We were just in time. We heard Father's footsteps on the landing, heard him open Johnny's door.

"Now, Flo, don't carry on so; you'll make yourself ill," Father's deep voice said. "Do you want to wake up the girls?" We hardly dared breathe. More steps, our parents' door closed.

I never forgot the sound of that weeping. And somehow it was all tied together—the sea, the moonlight, Mother's tears, and the awful knowledge that my little brother was never coming back.

Kathleen and I don't talk about that night. And I never got over feeling, deep down, that I was to blame for the accident, despite Mother saying I wasn't.

When I have a nightmare and cry in my sleep, my sister has to shake me awake.

"Johnny?" I ask, and sit up.

Kathleen puts her arm around me.

"You had a bad dream, Lou. Johnny's with the angels now."

There are times when something reminds me of him again–the way the sun glitters on the River Thames...Mother's anxious look if one of the young ones comes home late, after play.

It wasn't long before Father stopped delivering groceries for Mr. Dawson. Uncle Alf spoke about them going into partnership at Covent Garden, selling produce at his stall.

"You're my brother, Jack," Uncle Alf would say. "It stands to reason I want you as a partner. We're family, aren't we?"

I overheard Mother talking to Mrs. Bernardi from next door about it. "It's the pitying looks he can't stand. He doesn't want to be reminded. He'll do better with Alf. No one knows his fruits and vegetables like my Jack–he'll go when he's ready."

Uncle Alf came to see us one evening and brought a big round yellow piece of fruit from the market. He cut it up in wedges and gave Kathleen and me a piece each to taste. "Very popular with all the chefs, this is. They buy them to serve up for their lordships' breakfasts. Grapefruit, they're called," he said.

I watched Kathleen pucker up her mouth and run into the scullery. I licked my piece with the tip of my tongue. "It's horrible! I don't want it."

Mother slapped my bottom, not hard though! "Don't you be so rude to your uncle Alf," she said. "It's a special treat. Sorry, Alf."

Kathleen came back in, wiping her mouth. "It might taste better with a bit of sugar on top, Uncle Alf."

"Quite right. You are a clever one and pretty as a picture. So are you, Lou." He put a penny in the pocket of my pinafore. "Mind you share!" Uncle Alf said. "Come on, Jack, I'll stand you a pint, and we'll drink to our partnership: *Alf and Jack Gardener, Fresh Produce.*"

That year I started school, two years after Kathleen. Every day, we'd walk home together. One afternoon, instead of Mother waiting for us at the scullery door, Mrs. Bernardi stood by the kitchen table. She was buttering thin slices of bread and cutting them into triangles. She put them on the pretty flowered plate that Mother told us had been a wedding present. We never used it!

"You carry the plate, Kathleen, and Louisa can bring up the cup." Mrs. Bernardi led the way upstairs, holding the tray with our brown teapot, the milk jug, and a bowl of sugar.

Where was Mother? Why weren't we going to have our tea in the kitchen? We were never allowed to bring food upstairs.

Mother's bedroom door was open, and she was sitting up in bed. Mother was always the first one up and dressed in the morning, and her day did not end until long after we were asleep.

"There you are at last, my two big girls. I have a surprise to show you!" She held a bundle in each arm, tightly wrapped in shawls. "These are your new brothers. This is Harry, and this one is Tom. Aren't they beautiful?" Mother asked us.

"Twin boys!" Mrs. Bernardi said.

"Why are they all red?" I asked.

"They've been on a long journey in the doctor's bag, and they're tired. Now you go down and have your tea," Mother said.

"I've seen the doctor's bag–there's not room in there for two babies." Kathleen looked puzzled.

I saw Mother wink at Mrs. Bernardi, who said, "The doctor brought them one at a time." She and Mother looked pleased.

The boys' faces didn't stay red, but their hair did. They both have the same snub noses and identical freckled faces. Only Mother can tell them apart.

Thank goodness the next baby was a girl! She was born when I was nine. Emily is the image of Kathleen, with her auburn curls. Father's hair used to be red, too, before the gray crept in. Mother and I are fair, and I'm glad my hair is straight—it makes it easier to braid.

Mother said, "That's the last one, or we'll be eating and sleeping in shifts!" But after Emily, there was one more: Little George was born in 1910, the year our king, Edward VII, died, the year after I turned twelve and left school. Mother said she needed me at home to help with the children and the chores.

Who invented Mondays and Tuesdays? Every week I think the washing and ironing will never get done. I don't know whose shirts get dirtier or ripped more often—my father's or the boys'! And I hate touching raw meat before I put it through the grinder, to mince for shepherd's pie. But I love taking the young ones for walks and stealing five minutes with Mother for a chat and a cup of tea!

London, England

1910

2

"Life's not fair"

I 've been hoping and hoping that I can go out
to work like Kathleen. She found herself a job
the minute she left school. She got taken on at
Miss Jenny's Drapery, where she'd been going
every time she had the chance. Kathleen's been
crocheting and sewing and making clothes over
since we were little girls.

Mother and Father didn't seem the least bit surprised when she told them that Miss Jenny had
agreed to hire her, for three shillings a week. Last
Easter, Kathleen bought a few ribbons and bits of
lace from the Odds & Ends bin and trimmed all our
hats. She's doing what she loves best.

"I know I could earn a few pence extra as a finisher
in the blouse factory, but I'll learn more at Miss
Jenny's, won't I?" Kathleen asked. Mother said that

it was fine to begin with and told her that she could keep half her wages for herself. The rest goes into the housekeeping jar.

Since King Edward died on May 6, people are wearing mourning bands to show their respect. Kathleen says they are running out of black crepe in the shop.

She confides in me, though. "I thought I'd like working in a drapery shop, Lou, but there's no challenge in it for me—the same faces, people wanting the same bits of ribbon. And if a customer asks me for advice about a pattern, Miss Jenny sends me down to count stock. She's showing that she's in charge, but what would it hurt if she gave me a bit of responsibility for a change? If she'd let me arrange the window display, I'd soon get rid of all that fuss and clutter. And another thing— some of the girls I went to school with are earning five or six shillings a week!"

"But it's a start, Kath—you're earning money, and you're out of the house doing something different."

I long for it to be my turn. I wish I had a bit more gumption like Kathleen, the way she makes things happen—talking her way into Miss Jenny's without even telling Mother and Father until it was all arranged. I wouldn't dare!

The coronation will be held next year, on June 22, 1911. Mother says if George had been another girl,

she'd have named him after the new queen instead
of after the new king, George V. It's just as well he's
a boy, so he can share a room with the twins.

Kathleen does not think Queen Mary is as beautiful and stylish as King Edward's widow, Queen
Alexandra. People adore her and say she is still
the loveliest woman in London. But I like Queen
Mary, with her shy smile and delicate complexion.
Kathleen admires her "exquisite" taste in hats. I
had to guess what that word meant!

When Emily is asleep, Kathleen tells me how she's
got her life planned. Mine, too. She's like Mother and
Father—she doesn't ask me if that's the life I want!

"Miss Jenny's is a stepping stone, that's all, Lou,"
Kathleen whispers. "I won't stay there forever. One
day I'll open a hat salon and a tea parlor, so we can
serve tea and pastries to the grand society ladies—
after they've bought their hats!" She jumps out of
bed and swans up and down the room.

"May I be of assistance, your royal highness?"
Kathleen makes a deep curtsy. Emily stirs, threaten-
ing to wake up. I can't help laughing at Kathleen.
She jumps back into bed and tickles me until I beg
for mercy.

"We'll call the salon the Gardener Sisters," she
says.

"And who is going to serve your grand ladies and
make fancy pastries?" I ask her, knowing full well

she has decided that I am to stay in the kitchen. As if I don't spend enough time there already!

"You will, Lou. Naturally, you will be in charge of all that side of things. Emily can serve when she's old enough; you'll train her. You're ever so patient with the little ones."

I remind her that Emily won't be little forever, that she may have her own dreams, but Kathleen's lost in a make-believe world.

"We'll all wear black silk dresses," Kathleen tells me.

Silk?

Here I am, in the middle of a hot afternoon, day-dreaming just like Kathleen. Young George fusses, reminding me I'm supposed to put him down for his nap. I still have to cook carrots and parsnips to put in the cottage pie Mother is making for supper. Emily plays quietly under the kitchen table with her rag doll. I heat the water to start the vegetables cooking. Thank goodness our twins are not back from school yet!

"I'll take George upstairs, shall I, Mother?"

She wipes her hand across her forehead, leaving a streak of flour. "Thanks, Lou, I'm almost finished rolling out the pastry." She cuts a perfect circle, leaving a scrap for Emily to whisk off the edge and gobble down.

"Now where did that bit of pastry go?" Mother says. "Is that mouse back in my kitchen? I'll make a cup of tea before the boys get home."

I carry George upstairs, and he falls asleep at once. *How can I persuade Mother to let me go out to work too?* I've been teaching Emily to do all kinds of small chores. *Wouldn't it be better for me to bring in a bit of money to help with the rent?* Father says the landlord's raising it.

I go back downstairs. Busy as usual, I mop up spills, finish off the last of the week's ironing, and give the scullery a good sweep. Now I'm behind with the vegetables.

The stewing beef has been simmering on the stove all morning. I chop the last potato and add more onions because that's how Father likes his pie. Mother swiftly trims the now-tender meat before mixing it with the partly cooked potatoes, carrots, and parsnips and covering the lot with the pastry lid. She opens the oven door, and a wave of heat makes our kitchen hotter than ever.

I wipe down the table, dry my hands on my apron, and set out two mugs. The tea's steeped. Mother pours milk into the mugs and we sit down.

Now's my chance. I try not to sound too eager. I don't want Mother to think I'm not happy at home.

"A girl I know has been taken on at Black's Glove Factory, and the foreman asked her if she knows of any others wanting work. The pay's the same as Kathleen gets. I'd like to try. What do you think?" *There, I've got it out at last!*

Mother doesn't say anything. Her expression gives nothing away.

"Kathleen started work when she was my age, and you were younger than me when you went into service." Mother stirs her tea round and round. I hold my breath.

"Louisa, I can't spare you and that's the truth. You do more than your share, helping with the young ones and the chores. I need you at home for now—helping me the way you do is good training for when you go into service. That factory is no place for you."

I can see Mother's made up her mind, but I'm not giving up so easily.

"Mother, ever so many of the girls from school are working in factories. Mrs. Bernardi's granddaughters are at Pink's Fruit Factory, so why isn't a factory a place for me, if it's good enough for them?"

"You should hear what Rosa thinks of that. Those girls are barely fourteen years old. On their feet for ten, twelve hours a day, in a steamy room with no windows. They cough all the time, she says. They can't scrub the red stains off their fingers, however hard they try. The foreman's a bully and a brute. I won't have you exposed to the likes of him! You're too young. No, don't tell me about Kathleen again. I need you here for the present, and I don't want to hear any more. And there's the back door. Surely that's not Father home so early?"

He clumps through the scullery and stands in the doorway, looking at us. I can tell by the expression on his face that he knows something's going on.

"It's very quiet in here. Where's Emily gone—off to Spain, is she? I've time for a quick cup of tea, Flo, before I pick up my last load of cabbages." Father sits down, and I bring another mug and pour out his tea.

"Who wants this?" he says, taking a shiny red apple out of his pocket. Emily comes out from under the table and clambers onto Father's knee.

"What's Spain, Father?" Emily asks, her mouth full of apple.

"It's a country across the sea, where Uncle Alf and I get our oranges from, my little duck."

Mother sets Father's mug in front of him, stirring in a big teaspoon of sugar—the way he likes it. She doesn't say a word.

"Is something going on that I should know about?" Father asks.

Mother's face doesn't move a muscle. "Louisa wants to work in a glove factory. I've said no!"

"Father, let me explain!" I know it's hopeless. There's no way I'd ever persuade him once Mother has made up her mind. If I was Emily's age, I could wheedle the world out of him. But then, it wouldn't be about going out to work I'd be asking for, only a sweetie.

At that moment, the back door opens. Tom and Harry cross the flagstones I'd mopped only this morning. The twins are dripping blood–one from his nose and the other from a cut lip. Both their shirts are filthy and torn, and the pair of them look as if they're going to burst into tears. I'm ready to join them!

"What in the world? After all I've said, into the scullery. Lou, hand me that old towel, please," Mother says. "It's only a bit of blood. It looks worse than it is. Tom, stand still. If you're big enough to fight, you're big enough to put up with a bruise or two." Mother sounds harsh, but she doesn't mean it. She cleans their cuts gently.

As I rinse the blood and dirt out of the towel, Father comes into the scullery. "Alright, who started it?" He looks from one twin to the other.

The boys hang their heads.

"If I'd come home looking the way you do when I was your age, I'd have felt your grandfather's belt. And I'd have been sent to bed, without supper. I work hard to put those shirts on your backs, and now look at them!" He bends down to put his boots on again.

"Sorry, Father," they whisper.

"Sorry is not good enough. You've got too much

time on your hands, running wild the way you do. I don't know what they teach you in that school. As if there is not enough trouble, with the price of fruit and vegetables sky-high. I hear talk of strikes down at the docks. Women are throwing themselves in front of horses and demanding the vote. Whatever next? No one seems to know their place anymore.

"This Saturday, and every Saturday from now on, you'll both do a man's work. Great big boys of eight should be a help, not causing trouble!"

Father can't bear to see Mother upset. He's not angry about the boys fighting. He just wants everything to stay the way it is and he and Mother to decide what's best for me!

"You boys will be too tired, after you've loaded and unloaded a few sacks of potatoes at the market, to be thinking about fighting. Uncle Alf and I can do with some help."

"Yes, Father." The twins nudge each other, all smiles again.

"Good-bye, my little mouse," he says, patting Emily's cheek. "See you later, Flo." At the door, he turns back towards me. "You'll go into a factory over my dead body. No daughter of mine is going to slave over a machine and look like an old woman by the time she's sixteen. I won't have it. You'll stay home until we decide otherwise. Mother is always telling

me how she doesn't know how she'd manage without you!"

The door slams and George wakes up crying.

"Can we go out to play until bedtime, Mother?"
The boys look at her hopefully.

"Hand me your shirts and go upstairs. See if you
can keep George quiet for a bit, and then I'll see."
She shakes her head as they pelt up the stairs, pushing each other.

"Lou, Father's right, and one day you'll thank us
for it. Next year, maybe you can be spared, and then
we'll look round for something suitable. I'm going
to soak these shirts. Emily, it's time to put your dolly
away."

*I didn't really expect Mother and Father to say any-
thing different, but why can't I help out, like Kathleen?*

Miss Pringle told us last week in Sunday school
that there are many different ways to help in the
world. *What I'd like to know is, why is it always the
eldest who gets to do things first?*

Father says that life's not fair, but that there's always
someone worse off than you are. Know your place in
this world, and do the best you can. No one can ask
more of you than that!

*How am I going to know what my place in the world
is if I don't get a chance to take a look at it?*

London, England

1911

3

"Your turn will come"

"I've never known it to be this hot, so early in June. The milk's off, again. Emily, come out from under that table and pop round to Mrs. Bernardi's. Ask her if she can spare us some milk for tea, until tomorrow. And don't forget to say please and thank you. Here's the jug, mind how you go, that's my big girl," Mother says.

Emily, at four and a half, still thinks being sent on errands is a treat. She comes back in a few minutes.

"I never spilt a drop. Mrs. Bernardi's got a pretty plate with a picture of the king and queen on it, Mother."

"Has she, now? And who's going to see their majesties ride in a carriage?"

"Me!" Emily jumps up and down.

It makes me hot, just looking at her. The coronation is in three weeks' time, on a Thursday.

"I'm thankful they didn't choose wash day,"
Mother says. *Would the earth have swallowed us up
if they had?*

We are all going, even little George. As Mother
says, he won't remember anything, but it's fitting
the whole family pays its respects.

George will ride on Father's shoulders. I know he'll
love the bands. Father plans to leave at dawn and has
picked out a good spot along the route.

Kathleen and I are hoping to go to a band concert
in the park that evening. Mother says we'll take sandwiches and a thermos of tea. "Everyone in the city
will be out, so you'd better be ready. I'm not waiting
while you girls fuss over your hats," she says.

"Let's hope the weather stays fine. If everyone
brings umbrellas, it'll look like a funeral!" I tell
Mother. Imagine, if I was at work and earning
money, I could buy her a coronation plate, or maybe
a mug.

I slice the cold mutton for supper—the last of
Sunday's roast.

"There are cold potatoes and pickles for your father,"
Mother says. They're what we have every week; I
don't need reminding. I'm slicing the loaf when
Kathleen comes rushing in. She's all flushed, and her
eyes are bright. *What has she been up to this time?*

"Sorry I'm late, Mother. It's busy at the shop right now."

After supper, Mother takes the little ones off to bed. Kathleen rolls up her sleeves and washes the dishes; I dry and put them away. Father's gone out for his evening pint at the Black Hart.

When Mother comes back down, Kathleen asks, "Is it alright if Lou and I have a bit of a walk?"

"Off you go then, but don't be too long." Mother picks up her mending.

We walk down the street towards Vauxhall Bridge. As soon as we're out of sight of our house, Kathleen stops and grabs my arm. "I'll burst if I don't tell you, Louisa. I've given in my notice!" She's breathless.

"You haven't! Whatever will Father say? Kathleen Gardener, here I am, pining to go out to work, and you hand in your notice!" I must have spoken too loudly because anyone would think we were being followed, the way Kath shushes me.

"Not so loud—people are looking. Keep walking. Well, of course I'm going to tell Mother and Father... at the right moment."

"What made you do it?" I ask her.

"Last week, a customer left Saturday's *Daily Mail* on the counter. On Monday morning, I took the newspaper to tidy away. Miss Jenny was serving a particularly fussy lady, so I guessed they'd be occupied for a while. She sent me down to unpack some new stock, and that gave me an opportunity to look over the SITUATIONS VACANT. I'm always hoping for something better. There was one from a milliner who needed an apprentice. I tore out the address and asked Miss Jenny if I might leave half an hour early. When I offered to make it up next day, she let me go.

"Don't you think it was an omen that I'd worn my straw hat that day—the one I'd just finished trimming? Lou, the milliner has the most elegant establishment! We're going there now..."

Kathleen and I link arms and cross the street near the Church of St. Savior. As we pass the cabman's shelter opposite, we hear a whistle.

"Don't look up, Lou," Kath says. She sounds exactly like Mother. We turn onto Lupus Street and walk up to the corner of Glasgow Terrace.

"Here we are, *Madame Claudine's*." Kathleen points to the name above the shop. "Isn't that a beautiful name? It's French."

I stare at the window display: a delicate gray hat with a feather curling up from the brocade ribbon round the brim and a veil glistening with tiny pearls. The table is draped with a pearl-colored shawl, and a string of pearls lies gleaming between the folds.

"That's an ostrich feather." Kath preens, as if she'd arranged the plume herself. "Madame serves tea to her clients, or lemonade. Our dream come true." She sighs happily.

I am just the least bit envious, pleased for my sister, but it is her dream, not mine. "However did you get taken on in such an elegant shop, Kath?" I ask her.

"After I left Miss Jenny's and found the salon, I waited. A lady came out, followed by a maid who carried a gold-and-white striped hatbox. A chauffeur opened the automobile door, and they drove off. I took a deep breath, straightened my hat, and went inside. A lady wearing a white tunic over a black silk skirt came forward. Her hair was black and shiny, coiled into a perfect knot, and fastened with a tortoiseshell comb. She spoke to me as nicely as if there were a chauffeur waiting for me too."

"'May I be of service, Mademoiselle?'

"I curtsied before explaining that I had come about the position of apprentice.

"She asked my name and what experience I'd had. Then she wrote the answers down on a little note-pad, with a tiny gold pencil.

"I told her I'd always wanted to learn how to make beautiful hats and how much I admired the window display.

"'What is it you admire?' she asked me.

"'It makes me want to see more of your hats, Madame. It is as if you are offering a taste, instead of the whole meal at once.'"

How does Kathleen find the right words to say?

"'I'll work hard; you'll never be sorry. Please give me a chance, Madame. I want to learn,' I explained, and she seemed to approve of that.

"She asked me to take off my hat and to put it on the counter. She turned it this way and that and asked if I had trimmed it myself. She must have approved because she took me into the little back· room, where she works on her designs.

"What a muddle! There were all kinds of fabrics –lace and muslins, silks and ribbons–tumbled about on the shelves. She'd dropped pins on the floor, and the sewing machine had no cover on it. Miss Jenny would have had palpitations if she'd seen it. I said I'd straighten it up in no time at all.

"She waved her hands at me helplessly, jangling her bracelets, and shrugged her shoulders.

"'I have only recently opened the salon,' she said. 'I am an artiste, *naturellement* I create each hat uniquely for every one of my clients, but with no help...' I could tell that she has never had to clean or tidy up after herself. A proper lady she is, from Paris, France.

"I'm going to keep that place spotless. I'll make myself so useful that she'll wonder how she ever did without me! I am to start next week, and she will pay me a pound a month. That's a whole shilling a week more than Miss Jenny gave me. Twelve pounds a year, Lou!"

"What did Miss Jenny say when you told her?" I ask, when Kathleen finally runs out of breath.

"I don't think she minded. She said her niece wants to work in the shop. Well, she'll come cheap, seeing she's a relative. Miss Jenny agreed to give me a character reference, though Madame did not even ask for one!"

"You talked too much to give her a chance. I am proud of you, Kath." I give her arm a squeeze. "But you're going to have to tell Mother and Father, before they hear that you've given in your notice," I warn her.

"I will, tonight. Stay close by when I tell them, won't you, Lou? And, one day, we will have a salon of our own, the way we always planned...."

Father's sitting outside the scullery door smoking his pipe as we return to the house. He taps the ash out on the back steps and follows us into the hot kitchen.

Mother is just closing the oven door—she's been baking. I am beginning to dread what is about to happen—Father is going to be angry with Kathleen. It is too hot to have arguments tonight. It feels like the threat of a thunderstorm.

"I baked some sour-milk buns. Had a nice walk, did you, girls? Kettle's on the boil; make some tea please, Kathleen. Louisa, go up and tell those rascals

there'll be smacks if they're not in bed in five minutes," Mother warns.

The twins are wrestling on the floor. I grab Tom
by the waist and Harry by an arm. Managing to separate them, I shoo both boys into bed. George watches
us wide-eyed, standing up in his crib. He's started
to take his first steps. I never thought he would, the
way we all carry him around. Emily runs to his every
bidding, a willing slave.

"You'd better get to sleep, all three of you, before
Father comes upstairs," I tell them.

George puts his thumb in his mouth and lets me
tuck him in. "Lou, Lou," he says, and my stomach
turns over. He's our Johnny, all over again.

"No more shoving, Tom, I saw you. Keep to your
own side of the bed." I pretend to glare at the twins.

"It was Harry, not me!"

"I don't care which of you it was—stop it. Mother
said smacks if she hears another word." It's all I can
do not to burst out laughing at their antics. I close
their door.

Father's voice reaches me as I come downstairs.

"You've done what?" he bellows. He and Mother
are sitting at the kitchen table. The tea's poured.
Kathleen stands facing them. When I join her, Father
glares at me.

"I suppose you knew all about it, too? Children

doing as they please, money wasted on ribbons and coronations, and the working man is nothing, not even in his own home! I don't need another upset this month, what with the docks on strike, my fruit rotting in the crates, and crops withered from the heat. How am I supposed to make a living? And now, Madam here tells me she's handed in her notice. Where's your respect?"

I feel Kathleen tremble beside me. She's going to say something that will make Father angrier than he is already, I just know it.

"Father," I say, "I found out only a short while ago, when Kathleen said she was going to tell you her good news. She meant to surprise you, Father, because of all your worries. And Kathleen told me that Miss Jenny wanted to employ her niece. Relatives have to come first. It's like you and Uncle Alf, isn't it, Father? And didn't Kathleen mention how much she'll get paid? Twelve pounds a year!"

Father stirs his tea. "There's no need to stand up for your sister. Kathleen has a tongue in her head."

"I should have asked you first, Father. I do see that now," Kathleen says. "I wasn't planning anything. It was an...an opportunity. It's ever such a respectable place. Please don't be angry, I've always wanted to work in a milliner's."

"That's true, Jack. She sews and trims better than I can. She did wrong not to tell us, but she's sorry, aren't you, Kathleen?" Mother coaxes them both.

Kathleen's eyes are pleading. "I'm really sorry I upset you, Father. It won't happen again."

Father takes a sip of his tea and pushes the mug away. "I should hope not. Our daughter's got a mind of her own. Takes after you, Flo! Well, all things considered–pour me a fresh cup of tea, Lou, this one's cold–you've done very well. Mind now, I don't hold with not talking it over with us first, but it sounds a decent place, a step up. So we'll say no more about it, Kathleen."

"Good night, Father, Mother, and thank you both," my sister says.

I'm just about to follow her upstairs, but Father calls me back. *Is he still upset with me?*

"I've never heard you speak your mind like that before, Louisa. You're growing up. Now that doesn't mean I want you getting ideas, too!"

"No, Father, I won't."

Later in bed, with Emily fast asleep across the room, Kathleen whispers, "Thanks, Lou. You were ever so brave. Your turn will come. Father's old-fashioned, but it is 1911 and things are changing."

I think if I was truly brave, I'd have told Father right then that my turn is next. I do not want to wait forever!

4

A Letter

I've been helping out at Sunday school for two years now, since I was twelve. I bring the twins and Emily to give Mother a bit of peace on a Sunday afternoon.

Miss Pringle, our Sunday school teacher, is tall and thin. She always wears high-necked white blouses, with a bit of lace at the wrist. In summer, her long skirt is blue; in winter, black; and then she adds a shawl. Today the heat has made her nose shine, and I see beads of perspiration on her upper lip.

Miss Pringle is the third daughter of the vicar. She teaches reading, writing, and piano to a few little girls from the shopkeepers' families during the week. At the end of this year, she's going to live in another rectory, in Hampstead, as a governess. Kathleen thinks Miss Pringle is quite old, as much as thirty or more! "Love must have passed her by," she says.

Today, Miss Pringle announces a service of dedication, on the Sunday after next, in honor of the coronation of the new king and queen.

"I hope you will all attend, and bring your parents. Tea and cake will be served afterwards." At this, the children *ooh* and *ah*, and Miss Pringle puts her finger to her lips.

Little Joyce, from the end of the street, sits next to our Emily. The poor mite is the youngest of nine and never looks quite clean. Who knows when she last saw a piece of cake, if ever!

Miss Pringle talks about the meaning of dedication and about service and duty. A bee buzzes loudly at the back of the room; doors and windows are shut to keep out the heat. Heads turn—it doesn't take much to distract the children this afternoon. Suddenly, I have a dreadful suspicion. I look for my brothers—they are sitting in the last row of chairs, hoping to be first out the door the moment Sunday school's over! They gaze at Miss Pringle angelically, a look with which Mother and I are familiar. I catch one twin's eyes, signal my *you'll be in trouble* look, and the buzzing stops.

"Who can tell me the meaning of the word 'duty'? Arthur?"

"Is it like soldiers going off to war to serve their country, miss?"

"Very good, Arthur, you shall have a picture to place in your album." The children receive a religious picture from Miss Pringle for good behavior. At the end of the year, she awards a prize to the child with the most pictures.

Miss Pringle goes to the piano and begins to play a hymn: *Onward Christian soldiers, marching as to war...*

We join in, singing the familiar words. When it is over, Miss Pringle takes the older children for Bible study, and I read to the little ones. This Sunday, it is one of my favorites from the "Book of Mark."

Jesus blesses seven loaves of bread and a few fish, and, miraculously, there is enough to feed a hungry multitude of people, who have come from afar to hear him speak.

Miss Pringle dismisses the class punctually at three o'clock. She nods to me to open the doors. Heat and sunshine pour into the stifling hall. I'd been hoping we could leave a bit early today. Kathleen and I had promised Emily we'd take her to the park. She's often fast asleep before Kath comes home from work. I tidy up the chairs, and Emily helps me to put the hymn books in a neat pile.

Miss Pringle covers the piano with a dustcover. "Louisa," she says, "I would like to speak to you for a few minutes. Emily, sit down please and wait for your sister, like a good girl.

"I have been asked by a Mrs. Ransom, housekeeper

to Lady Rupert Milton of Chesham Place, if I know
of a reliable girl to recommend as a nursery maid."

*I hope she gets to the point soon—our afternoon will be
over if she doesn't hurry up!*

"I should like to suggest your name, Louisa."

I glance over my shoulder at Emily, who is swinging her arms and legs to create a breeze. Any second
now, she's going to stop being good.

"Well, Louisa?" Miss Pringle gives the dustcover
an impatient tweak.

"I don't know, Miss Pringle," I answer.

She sighs. "I thought you would be pleased. You
are quite good and organized with the children.
And as you are at home and not at work yet, this
would be an excellent beginning for you. Would you
like me to speak with your mother? Perhaps you feel
that you cannot be spared, is that it?"

I come to my senses. *Isn't this what I've been waiting
for?*

"It is very good of you to think of me, Miss Pringle.
Thank you—I would like you to recommend me for
the position."

"Very well, Louisa, I will tell Mrs. Ransom that I
have found a possible candidate. I will notify you
when an interview has been arranged. That is all,
Louisa. Good afternoon."

Emily talks, nonstop, all the way home. I scarcely
listen.

"Was I good, Lou? Can we see Kath now?"

"Yes."

What have I done? What will Mother say? How am I going to tell Father that I've agreed to apply for a position without asking him first? It might never happen... Lady Milton may not want to see me...someone else might have been found....

Kathleen's waiting for us. How grown-up she looks– longer skirts, a new hat! I am not going to tell even her. I'll wait until I have something to tell.

The note arrives after lunch on Tuesday, delivered by the vicarage maid. It is addressed to Miss Louisa Gardener. I have never received a letter before.

"Who was at the door?" Mother comes out of the larder, where she's been wiping shelves. She holds the long yellow flypaper, black with flies. *Ugh!* I shudder and look away from the sticky, writhing mess. Miss Pringle would say we are all God's creatures, no doubt.

"Throw it on the waste heap, Lou, please." Mother looks at my face and sighs. "Never mind–I'll take it. And you want to work in a factory? You'd not last two minutes, my girl. Where you pick up your finicky ways, I don't know."

When she comes back, wiping her hands, I haven't moved. I am almost afraid to open my letter.

"You haven't said who was at the door." Mother

looks over my shoulder. "Whoever can be writing to you?" she says, drying her hands on her apron.

"Miss Pringle sent it."

"Aren't you going to open it?"

I take a knife from the table and slit the top of the envelope.

"As long as it's not another bill, I don't mind what it is, or who it's from. Do read it, Lou. It can't be that big a secret if it's from the vicarage."

I read the letter aloud.

The Vicarage
The Grove
June 10, 1911

Dear Louisa:

I have spoken to Mrs. Ransom, who informs me that Lady Milton will see you on Friday morning, at ten o'clock. You are to present yourself at the servants' entrance of 4, Chesham Place. Please ask for Mrs. Ransom, the housekeeper.

I have enclosed a copy of the character reference that Mrs. Ransom will hand to Lady Milton.

With good wishes,
Yours sincerely,
Ida Pringle

Mother fans herself with the envelope. "Louisa Gardener, you have quite taken my breath away. An interview for a domestic position with titled folk, that's very good indeed. I've been thinking about looking around for something for you, maybe in a household with just two or three servants. Your father agreed. But a housekeeper! That means a cook and maids and even a butler." She sits down at the table. "Chesham Place? Father would know it–I believe it is near Grosvenor Road, by Belgravia Square. Father's old delivery route is near there. A very good address, my girl. For a start, we'll have to get you new boots. Your Sunday frock will do for the interview, but a lady will notice the state of your shoes.

"You'll have your bath on Thursday night instead of Friday, and no need to share the water with Kathleen. Pass me the jar on the mantel, please."

I hand it to her, and Mother takes out some coins.

"Two shillings should be enough. We'll go to the market stalls tomorrow and pick you up a pair of boots. I am pleased for you, Lou! We won't say any-thing to your father until after the interview–it can be a surprise." Mother kisses my cheek–she doesn't do that often now that Kathleen and I are growing up.

"What else does Miss Pringle say, Lou?"

I read again.

The Vicarage
The Grove
June 10, 1911

To whom it may concern:
   Louisa Gardener is a well-spoken girl with excellent manners. She attends Sunday school regularly at St. Margaret's Church, with her sister and brothers. For the past two years, Louisa has helped to prepare and tidy the hall before and after class. She is firm and pleasant with the children, to whom she reads and teaches hymns.

   Her presence is beneficial to the smooth running of the afternoon. She has shown herself to be trustworthy. I have no hesitation in recommending her as a nursery maid.

Yours truly,
Ida Pringle

"Now don't get your hopes set too high, Lou," Mother says. "There'll be other girls interviewed, though you're as good as any, if I say so myself! Mind you, it will be hard work, and there'll be strange rules to learn. They have different ways of doing things in a big household. You'll answer to the nanny for most everything...do all the tasks she's too grand to do!

"There are those who do the hiring and those who get hired. Once you're there, you'll find as many differences between the servants as there are between the lords and ladies and those who work for them. Downstairs is like upstairs: there have to be rules for those at the top and those at the bottom of the heap. Housekeeper and butler are at the top; the cook rules the kitchen; the nanny's the queen of the nursery. Maids all have different duties: the kitchen maid answers to the cook, the scullery maid does the rough work. Then there are downstairs, upstairs, and parlor maids, and footmen, too.

"For the interview, you'll bob a curtsy to the housekeeper and a deeper one to her ladyship. Answer when you're spoken to, and things will turn out just fine. I want what's best for you, Lou.

"Now we'll have a cup of tea.... I'll miss you, Louisa, more than you know, but you've earned your chance. You're a good girl, and you're old enough to leave home–it's time."

"I'll give you half my wages, Mother. I've been longing to help out, like Kathleen."

5

Number 4, Chesham Place

O n Friday morning, the sixteenth of June, at ten minutes to ten, I walk around to the back entrance of Number 4, Chesham Place. *What a big grand house this is!* I count five stories and I'm feeling over warm and scared. It's taken me an hour to walk here. I've time to catch my breath–I don't want to look as flustered as I'm feeling inside. *Why can't I be more like Kath?*

The toes of my next-to-new boots are covered with a layer of dust. That won't do–going into a fine house like this one unkempt. They'll think I'm slovenly! Mother made me wear the new boots all of yesterday to soften them, so I won't get blisters. I give the leather a quick dust with my handkerchief and wipe my hands, clammy with heat and nerves. I take a deep breath. Now, I'm ready to go down the wrought-iron steps and knock at the door.

A maid, dressed in a pretty striped dress and wearing an apron and cap, answers the door. "Good morning. May I help you?" she asks.

"I'm here for the interview; I'm to see Mrs. Ransom."

"You're expected. Come in. I'll let her know you're here."

She leads the way through a flagstone back kitchen, bigger than the whole of our downstairs. In the main kitchen, a girl kneels, polishing brass on a stove that takes up most of one wall.

"The girl's here about the position, Mrs. Porter."

A woman looks up from the pastry she's rolling out at a table, which is scrubbed white and seems long enough to seat half our street. I bob a curtsy and bid her good day.

"You look as if you've had a bit of a walk. Dean, hand the girl a glass of water, if you please."

"Thank you very much, ma'am." I drink, grateful for the kindness. Dean whisks the glass away from me the moment I've emptied it and goes out.

"I am Mrs. Porter, Lord and Lady Milton's cook," the woman says, deftly lining pie plates with the pastry. "You will be sent for shortly, and who might you be?"

"My name is Louisa Gardener, Mrs. Porter."

She nods, looking towards the maid who is still crouched in front of the stove.

"Time you finished blacking that stove, Roberts. Croft," she calls over her shoulder, "I'm waiting for those vegetables. We've salads to make up for the luncheon party. Sixteen, Mrs. Ransom said." She stares at me, her fierce blue eyes summing me up. It's a kind look, and I like her immediately.

Roberts gets to her feet, taking her rags and polish with her. She gives a sullen glance in our direction.

A young maid comes out of the larder carrying a basket of vegetables, which she puts on the table.

Mrs. Porter looks up at me. "You remind me of someone, someone I worked with a long time ago. If you don't mind my asking, what was your mother's maiden name?"

"Florence Partridge, before she married Father. He jokes about their names—'Partridge and Gardener go together,' he says." I'm so nervous, I'm talking too much. *Whatever must she think of me?*

A bell rings, one of a whole row set high up on the kitchen wall.

"That will be her ladyship waiting in the drawing room," Mrs. Porter explains.

The maid who let me in earlier appears at the door. "Mrs. Ransom says her ladyship is ready to see the new girl. This way, please."

I follow her out of the kitchen and along a flagstone passage, past a room where a man, wearing a black jacket, stands counting silver spoons.

"That's Mr. Briggs, our butler, in his pantry. The next room is Mrs. Ransom's parlor." We walk past more rooms, up some steps, and then through a green baize-covered door that swings shut, noise-lessly, behind us...up a short flight of steps and through a heavy oak door that opens into a hall. It is filled with sunlight, reflected in the chandeliers and the gold-framed mirrors, pooling, in gold flecks, on the polished floors. I wish I had time to take it all in.

Dean whispers, "What did you say your name is?"

"Louisa Gardener."

The double doors to the drawing room are open. She knocks, even so, and a voice calls out, "Come."

"Gardener is here, your ladyship."

I stand just inside the door, not certain what to do next. A slim beautiful lady rises from the desk by the window and crosses to the sofa. She is dressed in a summery gown of lavender muslin. I can't help staring at her sleek blonde hair, her elegant gray shoes, and the graceful, unhurried way she moves.

Vases of fresh flowers stand on small tables. Delicate ornaments and lamps are arranged close to each of the sofas. Chairs seem to be grouped together, as if just waiting for more beautiful people to sit, sip tea, and converse. The carpet is deep and soft, and there are flowered rugs scattered about. *What if my boots leave marks?* I can hear Kathleen's

voice in my head and imagine her laughing response:
"What do you think the servants are for?"

"Thank you, Dean. That will be all."

Dean disappears, closing the doors softly behind
her. Everything is quiet up here, not like down in the
kitchen with its hustle and bustle.

"Good morning, Gardener. Come closer."

"Yes, milady." I curtsy, waiting, my hands folded
together to keep them from trembling.

She glances at a letter. Even from where I stand, I
recognize the handwriting.

"I note that you have been assisting Miss Pringle
at St. Margaret's. What other experience do you have,
and how old are you?" she asks, adjusting the folds
of her gown. The sun streams in through the high
windows, despite gauzy curtains, which keep out the
worst of the glare.

"I will turn fourteen this month, milady. I help
my mother with the children and in the home. I
left school last year. My sister Kathleen, the eldest,
is apprenticed to a milliner. My twin brothers are
almost nine years old, Emily is four and a half, and
George was a year old in March."

"What, exactly, is it you do all day?" her ladyship
asks.

"Anything my mother says needs doing, ma'am.
I clean and dust, sweep and iron, help with the cooking, and keep an eye on the younger children."

"That seems quite satisfactory." She fans herself with a small ivory-handled fan.

"My husband and I have three children. Roger is seven, in his second term at boarding school. Portia is four, and Alexandra, two years old. Nanny Mackintosh, who has been with us since Roger was born, requires a reliable nursery maid."

"I am very fond of children, ma'am."

"In August, while my husband and I are abroad, Nanny and the children go to stay in the country, with my mother, Lady Portman. She may decide to accompany them to Folkestone, for some bracing sea air."

Folkestone's at the seaside. They'd not need me to go along, would they?

"Do you have any questions, Gardener?"

I've a hundred of them, but how can I ask when I don't remember a single name, or even how to find my way back to the kitchen!

"Very well, Gardener, Dean will take you up to the nursery now to meet Nanny Mackintosh and my daughters." She rings a bell. Dean appears, almost at once.

"Dean, take Gardener up to the nursery, please, then inform Mrs. Ransom that I would like to speak with her. Gardener will see her before she leaves. Make sure she finds her way. I am glad you are fond of children, Gardener."

I remember to curtsy and thank her ladyship before I follow Dean.

We go back the way we came, through the baize door. A maid in a cream-colored uniform, carrying a bouquet of roses, hurries past us.

"That's Hart, her ladyship's personal maid. I'm Annie Dean, parlor maid. But we are always called by our last names. Servants and children use the back stairs to the nurseries and upper floors. The main bedrooms are on the first floor, the guest rooms on the second, and the nurseries on the third. Croft, Mrs. Porter's helper, and Roberts, the scullery maid, sleep in the basement. I share a room with Hart, on the fourth floor. Mrs. Ransom, Mrs. Porter, and Mr. Briggs have their own quarters downstairs, next to the servants' hall." Dean leads the way up the uncarpeted, wooden back stairs to the nursery. "Here we are."

She opens and shuts the children's gate behind her, at the top of the stairs. The nursery door opens.

"Good morning, Nanny Mackintosh, this is Louisa Gardener. I'll be back for her in fifteen minutes, if that is convenient?"

"Very well, Dean."

I bob a curtsy to the woman Mother said is the queen of the nursery, hoping I will do!

Nanny Mackintosh's eyes, as brown as her uniform, inspect me from head to foot. I am determined not to lower my eyes, much as I long to do, and stare back. "Plain and solid, no nonsense about her," I know Mother would say with approval. Her salt-and-pepper flecked hair is pulled back from her pale face. Her mouth does not look as if it smiles much. Perhaps love has passed her by, like it has Miss Pringle. And, no doubt, she has a great deal of responsibility to bear.

She is dressed in brown from head to toe, except for her crisp, immaculate, white cap, cuffs, and pinafore. A timepiece is pinned to her chest.

"You may enter, Gardener. This is the day nursery. Thumb out of your mouth, Miss Alexandra." Nanny speaks with a soft burr, rolling her *r*. She whips the baby's thumb down.

What a lovely little girl, with golden hair like her mother! The baby sits in a high chair, playing with bricks on the wooden tray in front of her. She looks up at me, smiles, and drops a brick. I am familiar with that game and pick up the brick. I balance it on top of another. The child crows in delight and throws it again. I hear Nanny *tut, tut*.

"Do not encourage Miss Alexandra, Gardener. We never throw things in this nursery!" I put my hands behind my back obediently.

"Come and say how do you do, Miss Portia. No, leave your pencil on the table." The child puts her pencil back and stands beside Nanny. She looks down at her feet and whispers a greeting.

"Good morning, Miss Portia," I say. "I have a sister at home about your age."

"You have ten minutes before we get ready for our walk, Miss Portia," Nanny warns. "I believe in running a tight ship. I expect my orders to be obeyed, both by children and servants. Firmness and discipline above all, Gardener."

I am not sure if I am expected to answer. She seems to be waiting for me to say something.

"Yes, Nanny Mackintosh, I understand. I have three younger brothers and a little sister at home."

She continues to speak, so I seem to have said the right thing!

"We take the children out for walks, morning and afternoon. We go to Belgrave Square in the morning. After our one o'clock lunch and after the children's nap, we go further afield to Hyde Park, weather permitting, before tea."

"Yes, Nanny Mackintosh," I say.

"As nursery maid, you are to keep the day and night nurseries clean and tidy. They are to be swept and dusted before breakfast is brought to us at eight o'clock. In winter, the scullery maid lights the fire. She, or the footman, makes up the fire as needed.

"I began work, as a young lass, as a second nursery maid to a titled family in Scotland. I cleaned out the grates before breakfast and ran up and down for trays as well as coal. We knew what work was in those days!"

"Yes, Nanny Mackintosh. I am not afraid of hard work," I reply.

"That remains to be seen," she says, her mouth set in a thin straight line.

Older people always seem anxious to tell us how hard life was when they were young. *Do they think life is so much easier for those starting out now?*

A tall fireguard stands in front of the fireplace beneath the broad mantel. Winter seems far away. A rug lies between a comfortable, cushioned armchair and a rocking chair. The floor is covered with green linoleum, which is easy to keep clean. There are bars across the windows that overlook the square, a wide window seat, a bookshelf, a rocking horse, and a dollhouse almost as big as Miss Portia. I wish I could look at the little rooms and tiny pieces of furniture. A cretonne-covered toy box stands in a corner. *What wouldn't I give for our Emily to play here? She'd never leave that dollhouse–she's never even seen one!*

"The nursery maid bathes and dresses the children under my supervision. There is some light washing of the children's things and mending. Are you capable of doing that?" Nanny asks me.

"Yes, Nanny Mackintosh, I darn and hem."

"I require my morning tea punctually at 6:45. The nursery maid brings it up to me. All our meals are

eaten here with the children. The footman carries up
the heavy trays. After tea, if their parents are at home,
the children are taken downstairs to see them and,
on occasion, to meet guests, if Lady Milton wishes it.

"This way to the night nursery. Miss Alexandra has
recently been moved in with Miss Portia. The nursery maid sleeps in the small, adjoining dressing
room. The door is kept ajar at night, should the girls
require attention. Miss Portia had measles last year
and is not robust–she is a finicky eater. You are not
a heavy sleeper, I trust?"

*Does that mean I am to have a room of my own, if I
get taken on? What if I have one of my bad dreams and
wake up the children?*

"Oh, no, indeed, Nanny. I wake up at the slightest
sound."

"This is the children's bathroom. Staff have their
weekly bath in the servants' bathroom downstairs.
And this is Master Roger's bedroom. Nothing is to
be moved, nor may the girls play with his toys.

"My quarters are on the other side of the day nursery," Nanny says, looking down at her watch. "It is
time to get the girls ready for their walk. You seem
a sensible, willing girl, able to take instruction."

There is a knock on the door.

"Punctuality is a great virtue. Dean will show you
the way down. Good-bye, Gardener."

Dean and I walk down together.

"You are almost finished. There is a lot to take in, isn't there? Mrs. Ransom is expecting you." Dean points to the housekeeper's room.

"Thank you for showing me everything," I say.

"Good luck! I must hurry and help Hart get the table ready for the luncheon party."

I knock on the housekeeper's door, hoping I will make a good impression. *How will I ever remember so many instructions?*

"Come in, Gardener." I curtsy to her. "Lady Milton has asked me to speak to you regarding the position of nursery maid...."

Mrs. Ransom sits behind a big desk that has everything neatly placed for easy reach: paper and pens, pencils, two inkwells, a carafe of water, and a covered glass.

The wrists of her white high-necked blouse are cuffed with lace, and gold-rimmed glasses hang on a chain from her neck. Her hair is quite gray, though she does not look older than Nanny. Well, it's no wonder, with all these servants to give orders to and making sure they do everything right!

"Her ladyship has decided that you seem a suitable nursery maid for Nanny Mackintosh. She is prepared to give you a three-month trial. Wages start at eleven pounds a year, paid monthly by Mr. Briggs, the butler. This amount will be reviewed in a year's time, if you prove to be satisfactory. We provide uniforms for

our staff, made up by Mrs. Wilson, the household's
dressmaker. You will supply your own indoor and
outdoor footwear.

"Mrs. Porter serves a light supper of cocoa and biscuits in the servants' hall every night, at nine o'clock.
This will give you an opportunity to meet your fellow
servants. You will take Nanny's cocoa up to her,
unless she has it here with me.

"You may have one full day off a month and every
other Sunday afternoon, after lunch. Lady Milton per-
mits one evening out each week, if all your tasks have
been completed to my satisfaction. You may attend
Sunday morning or afternoon service, alternating
with Nanny Mackintosh. I will inform you which
days you attend which service, after I have decided
the month's schedule. All my under-eighteen-year-
old maids are to be home by nine and in bed by ten
o'clock. There is one week's paid holiday a year, and
you are allowed to spend Christmas Day at home
with family.

"You may move in the Saturday after coronation
day, on June 24th, after lunch. This will allow you time
to settle in and for Nanny Mackintosh to acquaint
you with your duties before you commence work the
following Monday morning."

She holds her pen poised over the inkwell. "This
is an exceptional starting opportunity for a girl of
your age. What shall I tell her ladyship?"

I am to be taken on? I did not really expect an offer so soon. Mother told me what to say, if I was asked.

"Please tell her ladyship that I am very grateful for the chance, thank you, Mrs. Ransom. I will do my best not to disappoint you or her ladyship."

First thing, I'll go and thank Miss Pringle for putting in a good word for me.

"Very well, Gardener. Any problems you encounter, you will bring directly to me. You may go now to get measured—the sewing room is across from my parlor. Good day."

What I'd like to do is to run home to tell Mother. I feel like skipping the length of the corridor, that's how happy I am! Instead, I hold myself straight and tall, smooth my hair, which I have put up for the first time for today, and go into the sewing room.

A tiny birdlike woman, looking old enough to be Mrs. Ransom's mother, turns a sheet. She wears a lace cap perched on her white hair. A gray-striped apron covers her black dress. The sound of the door closing makes her look up. She removes a pin from between her lips.

"So you're the new girl. The last one stayed barely long enough for me to let down her hems! Gardener, isn't it?" She takes the pencil from behind her ear and writes my name down in a thick ledger. She removes the measuring tape from around her neck and approaches me.

"Twenty-five years I've been sewing for the family–first for his lordship's mother and now for young Lady Milton. Hold still–staff hems are to be worn three inches above the ankle. Thirteen or fourteen, are you? Big hems then, to allow room for growth. You're a bit on the thin side, but you'll soon put on a few pounds with Mrs. Porter cooking. Now then, prints for morning, light blue, and for afternoon, navy blue. Caps and pinafores bought ready-made, not like the old days. Hold out your wrists." She mutters to herself and writes down measurements, clicking her tongue and shaking her head.

"I'm stronger than I look, Mrs. Wilson," I tell her.

"You'll need to be. Now there's a cape here somewhere, for outdoor wear. I can take it in a bit, make it good as new. There, you're done. Your uniforms will be ready when you start." She sits down at the sewing machine and begins to turn the handle again.

I thank her and go out in the passage, longing to lean against the wall for a moment. My head spins. I've been looked at and over, questioned, hired, given information, and introduced to more faces than I'll ever be able to put names to!

The girl who was cleaning the stove when I first arrived pushes past me, bumping into my shoulder. The look on her face makes me wonder if she did it on purpose. The corridor is plenty wide enough for her to get by, even if she is carrying a bucket and rags! I expect she is just tired of being at everyone's beck and call.

"So you're the new nursery maid, are you?" She looks behind her. "I don't give you long with Nanny Mackintosh." She sounds spiteful, so I don't reply.

"I'm on my way upstairs to give the nursery windows a clean before the old biddy returns from her walk. You'll be cleaning them soon. I've more than enough to keep me going downstairs."

A young footman, carrying a tray with coffeepot and cups, passes by. The butler emerges from the pantry with a decanter and glasses.

"Gossiping again, Roberts? I trust you have finished cleaning the nursery windows. I have no wish to have any more complaints from the nursery!"

"I'm on my way upstairs, Mr. Briggs. I was just giving the new girl directions to the kitchen." Roberts hurries away.

I hope that I won't have trouble from Roberts. If I'm lucky, I will not have much to do with her.

"Welcome to the staff, Gardener. You will find this a busy household. All of us have our own tasks to do, in order to keep the wheels of the household running like clockwork."

"Yes, indeed, sir," I say.

"Then I bid you good day, Gardener." He continues down the passage, and I return to the kitchen. I hope he does not think I was keeping Roberts from her duties. I do not want to start off on the wrong foot with him.

The kitchen door is open and I go in. Mrs. Porter is inspecting a vast silver platter, held by Dean. It is laden with tiny sandwiches, to which Mrs. Porter adds a final sprig of parsley.

"That will do, but come back as quick as you can. The lobster patties are ready to come out of the oven," Mrs. Porter says. I hold the door open for Dean.

"So you made a good impression and are joining us, Gardener. Not that I'm a bit surprised, seeing whose daughter you are! Tell your mother, Bessie Porter wants to be remembered to her."

I thank her, relieved to escape outside and think about all that has happened since I arrived. The clock on the kitchen wall said five minutes to twelve. The two hours I have spent here seem like two weeks! I feel glad and sorry, both. I'm proud to be hired, but a little scared too. *Will I last longer than the last nurse-maid? And how is it that Mrs. Porter knows Mother?*

That evening, after supper, after I have told Mother and Father every detail about the morning, I give Mother Mrs. Porter's message. Mother's "Oh, I never" is close to a scream.

"Bessie Porter...Jack, you must remember her? She

was second cook, and I was her assistant, in the kitchen of Mr. and Mrs. John Ross."

"I could hardly forget, seeing that's where I first met you, Flo. That head cook, what an ogre she was! 'No followers in my kitchen,' she'd say, when I made the deliveries. You were what—sixteen, seventeen? She couldn't stop us meeting, right, Flo?"

"That's enough, Jack," Mother says.

"What did I say?" Father asks innocently.

I look down at my plate so as not to laugh.

"Well, Lou, I could not be more pleased," he says. "Mind you, I'll miss you when you leave."

Emily gets off her chair and comes over to twine her arms around my neck. "Don't go, Lou," she sobs.

Kathleen slams the scullery door, drops her boots on the floor, and comes running in, out of breath. "Sorry I'm late—I thought Madame would never let me put the CLOSED sign up tonight. Every lady in London wants a new hat for the coronation." She collapses onto a chair. "My feet are blistered from running and fetching all day! Did you get the position, Lou? What's the matter, Emily?" she asks.

"I don't want Lou to go," my little sister says. Her chest heaves.

Kathleen jumps up and hugs me. "You got it! Oh, my clever, clever Louisa, I'm so proud of you!"

"I'm to start next week, after the coronation. And I'm to sleep in a room of my own."

There is a short pause, then Kathleen says, "I'll
have the bed to myself, won't I?"

I have not really thought about what leaving home
will mean. I will not be living in this house anymore...not sharing a room with my sisters–whispering, laughing together, and being comforted after a
bad dream! Kathleen and I look at each other and
burst into tears. Emily joins in. Mother wipes her
eyes on the corner of her apron.

Upstairs, George hears us and calls out. Emily
runs up, still sobbing, to settle him.

Father can't bear to see any of us in tears and goes
out into the garden to smoke.

"It's too far to walk home on my evening off,
Mother, but I'll be home for Christmas and for a day
once a month. It won't be so bad, will it? And a week's
holiday every year–that's good, isn't it?" I say.

"Did you leave me any supper, Mother? I'm fam-
ished," Kathleen says, her arm around my waist.
"Lou, once you know which evening you get off, I
can meet you halfway. We can have a walk." Kathleen
is still making plans for us, the way she always has.
How I am going to miss everyone!

6

Nanny Mackintosh

I, who have never known what it is to be home-sick, must wait a whole month before I can go home! On this first evening, seated at the table in the servants' hall, everyone seems to be looking at me—the new girl—and I can barely keep from cry-ing. I try to remember which name goes with which face. My cheeks grow hot when I'm spoken to.

Roberts, who does not hide her dislike of me, snig-gers. "Look at the new girl blush," she says.

What have I done to upset her? She doesn't even know me.

Mr. Briggs clears his throat. Heads turn to him, deferentially.

"Mrs. Porter, I am reminded that when I started out as a young footman, my hands shook so much, I spilled the port wine I was serving at dinner. I was certain I would be told to pack my bags," he says, with the glimmer of a smile.

"Why, that's nothing compared to what I did, Mr. Briggs. The day I was promoted to assistant cook, I over-salted the soup and it was sent back to the kitchen. The staff put me in my place, make no mistake! They teased me unmercifully. 'Don't forget the salt, Porter,' they said for days, before I sent another dish upstairs."

Mrs. Porter is kind. Nevertheless, it is all I can do to swallow my bread and cheese. The lump in my throat refuses to go away.

When it is time for me to go back upstairs and bring Nanny Mackintosh her cocoa and biscuits, it is almost a relief. Nanny takes one sip before handing back her cup.

"The cocoa is cold. Bring up a fresh cup and make sure it is hot this time, if you please."

I go down and ask for another. "I am sorry to disturb you, Mrs. Porter."

She makes no comment, but tells Roberts to wash her hands and be certain the milk is scalding hot. Roberts mutters under her breath, and Mrs. Porter gives her a look, which I pretend not to see.

Nanny Mackintosh's idea of training me in the running of her nurseries is to correct everything I do. She manages to find fault from morning to night! Each day she checks the windows, and if they don't squeak with cleanliness, I must do them again. She runs her fingers along the mantel, looking for dust. Heaven help me if I forget to put a toy away the second it has been played with. Her favorite refrain is: "That is not the way we did things at Norland College!" There is no end to what Nanny will not tolerate. On the evenings she takes her supper with Mrs. Ransom, she changes into a black silk dress, which makes her look sterner than ever.

I am given a list of instructions to do before I go to bed.

The first time I accompany her to the park, and before I am permitted to push Miss Alexandra's perambulator, Miss Portia holding on to the side, I have to show Nanny my hands. She tells me, "Nanny Gilbert and Nanny Pritchard are most particular whom their charges mix with, as indeed am I. You must always remember, Gardener, that we represent Lord and Lady Milton. His lordship sits in the House of Lords, and the highest standards must be observed at all times.

"Miss Portia and Miss Alexandra are permitted to play within a short distance of the bench, where we nannies sit. You will remain close by and watch that the girls do not become overheated or chilled, depending on the weather. They may at no time raise their voices, push the other children, or touch anything lying on the ground!"

I feel sorry for Miss Portia. She spends too much time forced to sit at the nursery table, staring at her cooling porridge, or being told to eat her crusts or clean her plate. No one at home wastes food–we can't afford to–and the boys never leave a crumb. They are always hungry. *But could Nanny not bend just a little and give Miss Portia smaller portions?* She is not five yet and small for her age.

Nanny will often begin a sentence with "When I was your age, Miss Portia, I'd have been more than happy to see a bit of honey on my porridge. Eat up now." And I watch the child's eyes fill with tears.

Once, I cut up her bread into fingers to persuade her to eat her crusts. "Shall we count how many guards there are at Buckingham Palace?" I asked her. I counted slowly, to give her a chance to eat one up, so that I could say, "I was sure there were six. Where can that guard have gone?"

Well, Nanny just about exploded. "Food is to be eaten, not played with, Gardener. You forget your place." One thing for sure, Nanny will make certain I never have a chance to forget mine!

When I finally get to see Mother and the children on my first day off, I feel as if I've been away for a year, not four weeks! I have all sorts of stories to tell them and never let on how much I have missed them all.

Mother tells me to keep clear of Roberts: "There's always one troublemaker in every household. Unhappy at being overlooked, maybe, bearing a grudge, or with troubles in her life outside the house. It's nothing to do with you and none of your making."

Mother always says the right thing. "There's going to be a storm tonight, look at that sky! It'll clear the air a bit."

"It's not only the weather that needs to change, Flo," Father says. "I've never known a summer to be this hot! I tell you, if this dock strike goes on much longer and the trains don't start running again, the country will come to a halt! Men out of work for weeks, mines closing, and no money coming in to feed hungry families. What am I supposed to sell on the stall? Vegetables are drying up in the fields.

"Don't mind me, Lou, I am pleased to see you. Are they treating you fair? Getting enough to eat, are you?"

"I am, Father. Nanny Mackintosh is overstrict, but from the little she's said, I think she had a hard upbringing. Some of the servants are nicer than others. Mr. Briggs read us the obituary column last night–four more deaths from heatstroke. Do you know that he irons the *Times* every morning? We are to go to the country in two days' time to stay with Lady Milton's mother."

I don't mention that I might have to go to the seaside for a few days. It doesn't bear thinking about, what with Miss Alexandra liking to wander off if she's not watched all the time. *Suppose she falls into the water?*

I look up and see Mother's face. She seems a bit sad. *Is it because I'm going away, or because of all she has to do, or because of her worries about money, or is the heat getting her down?*

"You will enjoy the countryside, Lou, all that lovely green grass and shady places to rest."

I don't expect Nanny will let me do much resting, but I have so much now—my own room, food served up to me three times a day, and pay at the end of each month!

All of a sudden, hailstones, round and hard, rattle the window, followed by great drops of rain. We rush to close the door before the scullery floor is awash.

"That's what we need, days and days of rain," Father says, a pleased smile on his face.

"I'd best be on my way. I've to be in by nine o'clock." I kiss them all and give Emily and the boys a penny each from my first wages. Then I put some coins in the housekeeping jar.

"I'm sorry you missed Kathleen, dear. She had to work late tonight." Mother kisses my cheek.

"I'll send you a picture postcard from the country, Emmy!" I say as I hurry out.

The rain's easing off a bit, but the wind comes up, blowing my cape around me. I almost crash into Kathleen, who is just turning the corner into our street, her hair stuck in wet wisps to her cheeks. We hug each other, and I wish we had time to talk.

"I'm late, Kath. Mother will tell you everything. We're going away in two days, but I'll be back at the end of August. See you then! I get in trouble if I'm back late."

"I'll save all my news for you then, Lou. Miss you!" My sister blows me a kiss, and I run off, my shoes squelching through the puddles.

For the next twenty-four hours, I don't have time to think about anything except the packing. Nanny makes me start over twice, so she can show me how she wants the children's clothes folded. You'd think we were going across the ocean, not on a short journey to the country! Mr. James Harris, his lordship's valet and chauffeur, is going to drive us down. He drove Lord and Lady Milton last week, so they could spend time with her mother, Lady Portman. Mr. Harris wears an elegant uniform, dark blue with gold buttons.

Miss Portia and Miss Alexandra are excited at the hustle and bustle, and I am quite worn out from running errands and fetching and carrying for Nanny. As usual, whatever I do is not enough to please her!

Last night, Miss Portia was sick and I had to change her bedding twice. I will say this though: Nanny got up as soon as I called her.

"There is no need for the doctor. Miss Portia has always been high-strung," she says and goes back to bed!

I'm almost sick with nerves myself–another big house and staff to get used to, and Nanny tense and irritable in case the children are not on their best behavior. Miss Alexandra has a back tooth coming in and is whiny. She sucks her thumb for comfort and I haven't the heart to stop her, though Nanny insists it is a bad habit that must be broken. The place she trained at must have rules and regulations as long as my arm!

The great day arrives at last. I sink into the backseat of the motorcar, which Nanny informs me is a Rolls-Royce. It is almost big enough to live in. Mr. Harris has polished the chrome and glass to mirror brilliance, and the black paint shines so much, it sparkles. I have never been inside an automobile before.

The servants come out to wave good-bye. I feel like a queen, setting off in her carriage. How I wish Tom and Harry were here to see me!

Nanny Mackintosh sits in front, next to Mr. Harris. The children are in the back, one on each side of me. Nanny fans herself and sighs deeply.

"I have no great faith in the motorcar," she pronounces, as if she were going to her doom. She takes the smelling salts out of her oversized bag.

"It will be cooler once we get outside London," Mr. Harris says.

I would like the journey to last forever. Miss Alexandra falls asleep, happily sucking her thumb, and Miss Portia leans against my arm and dozes.

Amersham, England

1911

7

A Moonlit Garden

We arrive at the outskirts of the village of Amersham and soon reach Lady Portman's home. Tall trees and ornamental hedges surround the entire grounds. On either side of the wrought-iron gates, massive stone lions stand on guard. Mr. Harris drives up the long and winding driveway to a spacious, gabled, white house. The grounds are as beautiful as a park, with their flower beds a riot of colors. A gardener and his boy raise their caps, and the children, both wide-awake again, wave back happily. The front door is open. The butler waits on the steps to usher us in.

The housekeeper greets us and leads the way upstairs, to the nursery wing. "How very nice to see you again, Nanny. You do remember where everything is, don't you? Ellis will help you get settled, and tea will be brought up when you ring. Lady Portman and Lord and Lady Milton will see the children in the drawing room after tea."

Our luggage follows, carried up by a footman and a maid. It is all very grand, but gracious and welcoming. I feel comfortable immediately.

In no time at all, the children are tidied and seated at the nursery table. With the maid's efficient help, I have put most of their clothes away. I am informed I will share a bedroom in the night nursery with the girls. Nanny's room is on the far side of the day nursery.

All the nursery rooms are bright and sunny. The windows overlook the extensive gardens and the fields beyond. I point out a swing to Miss Portia, which hangs from the thick bough of a sturdy oak tree. She looks up pleadingly and I smile at her, wondering if I, too, might...no, Nanny would frown and think it unseemly!

"Open the door, Gardener. Are you dreaming? I rang for tea; it has arrived!" Nanny is out of sorts from the long drive.

The footman and a maid bring in our tea, setting out plates with a variety of tiny sandwiches. There is brown bread and butter, a cut-glass dish filled with homemade jam—from strawberries grown on the estate, the maid informs Nanny—scones, thick cream, biscuits, and a perfectly iced sponge cake!

Nanny's face registers her disapproval of this lavish spread. The door has hardly closed before she says, "There is far too much rich food! Quite unsuitable for the girls." Nanny rolls her *r* so that the word sounds like *girrls*. "And what is it that you find so amusing, Gardener?"

"I was thinking how prettily the table is set, Nanny," I say, trying to placate her.

"I predict that we will have two spoiled little girls to deal with when we get back to London. However, as it is only for a month, I'll say no more. Miss Portia, there will be no cake or jam until you have finished your piece of bread and butter. Both jam and butter, unheard of for children, even for a Sunday tea in my day!"

I tie a serviette around Miss Alexandra's neck and take a sip of the good strong tea, but not before I hand Nanny Mackintosh her cup. I know exactly how she likes it: a generous helping of milk and two heaping teaspoonfuls of sugar, though she says sugar is bad for children and growing girls, meaning me! She stirs her tea, tastes it, and moves the cake stand out of the children's reach.

"Most welcome, I am sure," Nanny says, pushing her cup towards me to be refilled. For once, she has no more complaints.

I just have time to wash the children's faces and hands before the parlor maid tells Nanny that the family is waiting to see the girls. "Lady Portland wishes Gardener to accompany you, Nanny Mackintosh."

We follow her down the back staircase and into the drawing room, decorated in the palest blues and greens. Glass doors lead onto the terrace, where the family is gathered. Lady Milton opens her arms for the children to run to her. I let go of Miss Alexandra's hand, and she toddles towards her father. Lord Milton lifts her high in the air.

Behind me, Nanny says, "Not after tea, your lordship, if you please."

He immediately sets his daughter back on her feet. She clings to his legs. "More, want more!" she shouts.

Nanny looks daggers, and I draw Miss Alexandra aside and whisper that she must not be so loud. Lord Milton asks his daughter if she has been a good girl and then tells her she may sit on his knee.

I am quite taken aback to hear Lady Milton say, "I do believe we have finally found a nursemaid who lives up to your high standards, Nanny Mackintosh. You may leave the girls with us for half an hour while you settle in. Gardener will bring them upstairs for their baths. We will come to the nursery later to say good-bye before dinner. We shall be leaving early in the morning to fetch Master Roger from school. He will spend his holiday abroad with us."

I stand a little way apart, but close enough to remove the children when their parents wish me to. They are exceptionally well behaved this afternoon, and Miss Portia leans fondly against her grandmother's knee. But after a while, Miss Alexandra begins to cry. Her tooth bothers her and the thumb is back in her mouth.

"Upstairs to Nanny, please, Gardener," Lady Milton says. "I will bring Miss Portia up presently." I bob a curtsy and carry Miss Alexandra upstairs. I can't help wondering what Lady Milton would do if she had to look after six children, without help, as Mother does. But then, we'd all be out of work.

"Miss Alexandra seems a little feverish, Nanny Mackintosh. My mother always swears by chamomile tea for sore gums." The moment the words are out of my mouth, I wish I had not spoken them.

"Indeed, Gardener. Do not imagine that because you overheard one compliment, this entitles you to run my nurseries, or to give me the benefit of your advice!" Nanny bristles.

"I beg your pardon. I spoke out of turn, Nanny Mackintosh."

"I trust it will not happen again. There can only be one person in charge. In future, try to learn from the experience I pass on and keep silent until your opinion is asked for."

"Yes, Nanny Mackintosh."

"Go downstairs and ask Cook if we may have a small pot of chamomile tea, also a teaspoon. Hurry up, and when you return, run a warm bath for Miss Alexandra."

I don't know where the door to the servants' quarters is. Thankfully, I encounter Ellis, the maid, who helped me unpack earlier.

"Do you require anything, Gardener?"

"Nanny sent me down to ask for a pot of chamomile tea and a teaspoon for Miss Alexandra, who is teething. I'm afraid I don't know where the kitchen is."

"I'll bring it up directly. Please tell Nanny she may ring the bell for whatever she needs. But I'll show you how to get to the kitchen. Turn right at the bottom of the back staircase, and the door is next to the gong stand. That's the servants' entrance, down the corridor and you'll find us!"

When I return upstairs, Lord and Lady Milton are in the day nursery.

"Look, Portia, here is Mama's old piano." Lady Milton sits, plays a few bars, and stops. She glances at the bookshelf. "I used to read some of those storybooks when I was only a little older than you are now."

"Will I read soon too, Mama?" Miss Portia asks eagerly.

"Quite soon. When you are five, you will share a

governess with some other little girls and go to their house every morning for lessons. And now, Papa and I must leave. We will send you a pretty postcard from France and see you in a month's time!

"Nanny, my mother has decided against taking the girls to the seaside. She feels that it will be over-crowded with day-trippers at this time of year. Lady Portman says she has heard there is a lot of whooping cough about! The country air here will be far more beneficial for the children." I am reprieved!

"Promise me, Portia, that you will be very good girls for Grandmama."

"Yes, Mama, good as gold." Miss Portia, overexcited at all the attention she has received, starts to run around the nursery table. I catch her and put my finger on her lips.

Miss Alexandra wriggles down from her father's arms. He keeps hold of her hand.

"We must dress for dinner. Come along, Rupert."

Lord Milton hands Miss Alexandra to Nanny Mackintosh. "We leave the children in your excellent hands, Nanny," he says.

After the door closes behind them, Nanny Mackintosh looks relieved to have the nursery under her command again. *Is she so disagreeable because she is anxious about her position?*

"Run the children's baths, Gardener. We must establish our normal routine before the children get quite out of hand. I shall have to have a word about plain food for nursery meals."

I run the bathwater, humming with joy. We will not be going to the seaside after all. I did catch a glimpse of a lily pond when I was on the terrace, but the girls will not go near without my holding their hands!

The days pass by too quickly. Cook takes little notice of Nanny's instructions about simple food, except for bread and milk at bedtime. Lady Portman reads a story to the children every evening, in the drawing room after tea. Miss Portia tells me it is about a naughty rabbit called Peter.

Ellis and I have some walks in the evening, after we complete our tasks. I cannot get over the beauty of the country lanes, with their profusion of wild-flowers and berries changing colors in the hedge-rows. Red squirrels play in and under the trees. I have seen a deer, and Miss Portia has spotted a rab-bit at the end of the garden. She calls him Peter Rabbit and tries to catch him! She makes for the swing at every opportunity, and I am secretly envi-ous. We play in the gazebo, and the footman brings us lemonade and biscuits midmorning. This must be what paradise is like!

When I take the children out in the garden after breakfast, the gardener feeds us strawberries by the handful. He shows them the grapes growing in the greenhouse. I ask him to speak to Miss Portia and Miss Alexandra about not going too close to the pond. He is most helpful.

"There are frogs and their babies in the pond. Don't you go too near, missies, and frighten them. But at night you will hear the frog mother and father sing to them."

So every night, after I have tucked the girls up in their beds, I open the window and let them listen to the parent frogs sing to their babies. And every night, Miss Portia says, "I can hear them *croak, croak.*" I am careful to close the window after a few minutes, as Nanny does not approve of night air!

She has developed a new habit since we've come here. Several times, late at night, I hear her footsteps, back and forth in the nursery. *Why?* So far, she has not ventured into our bedroom, but one never knows with Nanny Mackintosh!

It is our last day. A whole month has gone by and Lady Portman takes the girls out in the horse and carriage for a picnic. This allows me to finish packing. By the time Nanny brings the children back to the nursery, it is completed. Nanny can find no fault with me!

The children have been asleep for hours, but I am restless. It is too warm in the night nursery. The house has long settled. Hoping for a breath of cool air, I get out of bed, open the window, and drink in the sweet fragrance of the breeze. The garden beckons to me, as always: tonight—our last in this lovely, lovely place—more urgently than before.

On impulse, I rearrange my bedding to look as if I am lying, fast asleep, under the coverlet. I creep out to the landing. Holding my breath, I stand motionless, listening. Nothing stirs. I tiptoe downstairs, past the gong, careful not to brush against it in case its deep tone raises an alarm, then safely through the baize door into the servants' domain, just like at Chesham Place.

My bare feet make no sound in the long corridor. I enter the kitchen and pass the stove, still warm from tonight's farewell dinner, through to the whitewashed scullery. At the sink, I fill a glass to the brim with cold water and drain it to the last drop, careful to rinse the glass. I savor the coolness of the flagstones on the soles of my bare feet. I must not linger more than a few moments. *But what harm would it do to take just one last look…?*

The latch on the back door lifts easily, and I am outside at last, free to breathe in the sweet-smelling night. Mint and thyme, lavender and rosemary perfume the air. From every direction, the scent of late-summer roses reaches me. A breeze tugs at my nightgown and blows gently through my hair.

I promise myself that I will stay just long enough to try the swing, which I have ached to do from our first day.

I run through the long grass, reach out for the swing, sit and push myself off. Slowly at first, then faster and higher, I fly into the night. My white gown billows around me. Up and up I go, into the starlit sky–a caged bird released from its cage. Alone in the peaceful dark, I hear no voice to remind me of my place! Nearby, the turreted gazebo gleams like a great ship on a still sea of grass. Now and then, there is a ripple as the breeze skims the surface.

I close my eyes to feel the touch of the breeze on my skin more intensely, to breathe in the scents of the garden more deeply, and to listen more carefully to the whisper of foliage. *Do the trees and flowers ask each other about the strange white bird that intrudes into their kingdom?*

A voice reaches me from the shadows: "Open your eyes, you foolish, irresponsible girl. Return inside, where you belong!"

I look around, behind, then towards the house. *Is that a face looking down at me? Did the curtains twitch? Is someone else unable to sleep tonight?*

The swing slows to a stop. The moon, hidden until now behind the clouds, appears, shining more brilliantly than the stars. The garden is illuminated as though lit by a hundred candles. They draw me down the path towards the pond. The lily pads, their faces yellow-centered, gaze longingly up at the sky.

Moonbeams in ever-widening circles skim the water around them. Frogs begin their nightly dirge–a keening sound. I crouch down in the grass, afraid, my hands over my ears. I don't want to remember how my sister and I listened to cries we once believed were made by ghosts!

I force myself to stand, to turn my back on the moonlight and the voices in the pond, and return to the house.

Did you call out to us, Johnny, before your small body was dragged down under the water? Why didn't we hear you? I am sorry, I will always be sorry! I'll never forget.

I run back up the path, away from the moonlight shining on the water, away from ghosts that still haunt me. *If only I were dreaming...if only Kathleen were here to wake me and comfort me!*

I reach the door at last. I should not have left the children. I replace the latch and lean against the scullery door for a moment. I have wiped my feet so as not to leave marks on the clean floor. No one has seen or heard me. In a moment, I will be back in my bed. The moon distorts everything–sights and sounds in the dark, which in daylight seem nothing.

I go through the baize door and up the stairs. Nanny Mackintosh stands, looking down at me, waiting.

"Did you think you were unobserved? I watched

you, behaving like a creature, demented! Have you come to your senses at last? I had hopes for you, Louisa Gardener. I see I was mistaken. All my efforts to tutor you, my words of wisdom learned painfully over the years, have been wasted. Willful girl, how dare you go outside improperly clothed! Look at your hair, your bare feet! I should dismiss you on the spot!"

"I am very sorry, Nanny Mackintosh. I had a nightmare, I couldn't breathe, the heat..."

"Go in and sit; do not move!" She disappears and comes back holding a spoon and a large bottle of castor oil. Outwardly meek, I force down two spoonfuls of the evil-tasting liquid. I know better than to refuse. This is the worst punishment I can think of!

"A touch of heatstroke and overindulgence in rich foods may partly explain such an exhibition. Never, in all my years of service, have I encountered such unseemly behavior from a member of my staff! Get to your bed. We depart for home immediately after breakfast. I will decide how you are to be dealt with in due course!"

She watches me until I am back in the night nursery. The girls sleep peacefully; I kiss their cheeks. They are already dear to me. *Will I be dismissed?*

After I hear Nanny's door close, I open my window one last time. There is no moon now, and the frogs are silent. I fall asleep to the steady breathing of the little girls.

I cannot eat my breakfast, though Cook has sent up boiled eggs for a special treat. I nibble a piece of dry toast, dreading the long journey back to London. Nanny looks very pleased with herself, whether it is because she will once more be in charge of her own nurseries, or because she believes she has quenched my spirit, I do not know.

Mr. Harris has arrived and stowed the luggage away. The gardener hands him a basket of fruit and vegetables to give to Mrs. Porter.

Lady Portman kisses both little girls good-bye. "I shall miss you, my darlings. I hope to see you again very soon." She turns to Nanny. "My dear Nanny Mackintosh, what would we all do without you? I am so pleased that your nursemaid has adapted so well to your methods—a most suitable choice! We will look forward to your visit next summer."

"It is kind of you to say so, Lady Portman," Nanny says, looking gratified. There is even the glimmer of a smile. At least the corners of her mouth turn up, ever so slightly.

London, England

1912

8

Roberts

I have been with Lord and Lady Milton for over half a year. The preparations and the excitement of the Christmas and New Year festivities are over. Everyone is exhausted, particularly the servants. There was a puppet show for Miss Alexandra's third birthday; then a visit to the theater, with three small friends of Miss Portia's and their nannies, in anticipation of her fifth birthday. I could not help laughing when Miss Portia told me the nanny in the play *Peter Pan* was a dog! Who could have imagined such a thing?

However, when I caught Miss Portia about to jump off the nursery table in an attempt to fly like Peter Pan, Nanny banished her to the corner for half an hour. "If this ever occurs again, Miss Portia, it will be the broom cupboard for you!" Nanny meant it too.

The highlight of the season for me was our Christmas party, held in the servants' hall on Christmas Eve. We pulled crackers and wore paper hats. Mr. Harris played the piano, and Mrs. Ransom danced with Lord Milton. So did Mrs. Porter! Nanny, festive in her black silk dress, danced with Mr. Briggs! To my surprise, Charlie Phipps, the footman, asked me to dance. I did not think he had even noticed me! I had never danced with a young man before. Each of the maids got a length of beautiful material, and Mrs. Wilson will make up new Sunday dresses for us all.

We had the most wonderful time at home on Christmas Day. I had missed the family, despite getting to see them once a month on my day off. It was not the same somehow, hearing about the news instead of being a part of it all...looking at the twins making excuses for their latest piece of mischief, or watching our little George take his first steps, or having a quiet cup of tea with Mother when the washing and ironing were finally done for another week.

I do miss sharing a room with my sisters. But I am settled now at Chesham Place and have come to enjoy the life upstairs and downstairs. Most of all, I like feeling grown up and independent and proud, too, when I can put a few coppers in the housekeeping jar!

Mother cooked a goose for our Christmas dinner. Emily found the threepenny bit in her slice of Christmas cake, and Father brought home a pineapple from the stall, which was only a bit bruised. There was an orange for each of us, too. Kathleen and I had time to tell each other all that we had been doing. I am almost as tall as she is now!

It is bitter cold, and it takes me a long time each day to stuff the children into the many layers of warm winter clothing they must wear. Two pairs of stockings each, both cotton and wool. Nanny's only concession to the cold is to shorten our afternoon walks.

This morning, I am just getting the girls ready for their walk, when Dean asks Nanny to come down immediately to see Mrs. Ransom. Nanny removes the key that unlocks the gates to Belgrave Square from the hook hanging above the mantel. She hands it to me, as though it were some precious heirloom. I am surprised she does not warn me not to lose it. *Has she begun to trust me at last?*

"Return in one hour, Gardener. There is snow in the air."

The first snowflakes begin to fall shortly after I have unlocked the iron gates of the small square. I spot two robins fighting over a crust on the frost-tipped grass under the great oak tree. But the children are too excited by the first snowfall of the season to keep still, and the birds soon scatter. Miss Alexandra has not seen snow before and screams with delight. I promise the girls that if the snow does not melt in the night, I will let them make a snowman next day. Meanwhile they content themselves with putting out their tongues–normally forbidden–to catch flakes, which fall more heavily by the minute.

After our walk, we return home precisely on the hour to see a white-faced Nanny Mackintosh being helped into the new Daimler by Mr. Harris. He drives off quickly. Nanny does not turn round to wave to us, but sits with her head bowed. *What has happened?*

I am on my way upstairs when Dean stops me. "I am to take the children to the nursery," she says. "Mrs. Ransom wants to speak to you."

Mrs. Ransom is writing notes on her meticulously tidy desk. She looks up as I come in. "There you are, Gardener. You have just missed Nanny Mackintosh. She has received some bad news, I am afraid. Her father passed away unexpectedly." The big clock, which stands in the corner of her parlor, seems to tick louder than usual.

"Mr. Harris is driving Nanny to the railway station to catch the afternoon train to Scotland. She will be away for at least a week. Lady Milton has decided that you are quite capable of managing the girls while Nanny is in Edinburgh. Roberts will take over your usual cleaning duties in the nurseries. This will enable you to maintain the children's normal routine. Lady Milton will see the children after tea, in the drawing room, for an hour. Any concerns, Gardener, during Nanny Mackintosh's absence should be immediately brought to my attention. That is all."

I am dismissed. Nanny has never mentioned her parents. I wonder if her mother is still alive. I am very sorry about Nanny Mackintosh's loss, but a whole week without being found fault with will make a pleasant change! I can sit in the rocking chair by the fire and dream of what it would be like to be always in charge of the nursery....

Mrs. Porter sends up a delicious lunch of chicken and rice, and Miss Portia clears her plate. The snow has sharpened her appetite. Roberts comes in to take our tray without as much as a thank-you to me for stacking our dishes.

"You know what they say?" she says, smiling maliciously. "When the cat's away..."

I pretend not to understand and get up to open the door for her.

She mumbles a word I hope the girls have not heard. I shut the nursery door firmly behind her.

"What cat is gone away, Gardy?" Miss Portia asks.

"Roberts was joking–there is no cat here. And who might Gardy be?"

"That is going to be my name for you! What do your mama and papa call you?"

"At home, I am Louisa, or Lou."

"May I call you Lou?" Miss Portia wheedles. She is trying me out, in Nanny's absence. I shall certainly not do anything that I know Nanny would disapprove of, except to play with the children a little more now that Roberts will be cleaning my windows. I had better show Miss Portia that we are going to adhere to nursery rules.

"You know the answer to that, Miss Portia! Would you call Nanny Mackintosh Margaret?"

She wraps her arms around my waist lovingly. "You are funny, Gardener," she says.

I put the girls down for their afternoon rest and make sure the nursery is tidy. It snows so hard all afternoon that I keep the girls indoors and let them play with their new toys.

Next day, the sun comes out after lunch, and we are able to take our usual walk. When we reach our accustomed bench in the park, the nannies make room for me between them.

Before I sit down, I tell my charges they may play. "Look, Master Harold and Miss Diana have begun to make a snowman. Ask nicely and I am sure they will let you help."

"Why, Gardener, all alone today I see? I do hope Nanny Mackintosh is not indisposed." This is the first time I have been acknowledged with more than a polite nod or a good-afternoon in the eight months I have been coming here with Nanny Mackintosh.

Nanny Pritchard rises. "Master Harold, if I see you push your sister again, we will go home and you will be sent to bed without any tea," she says. She sits down again and includes me in her conversation with Nanny Gilbert.

"It is high time that young man was sent to boarding school. He is getting quite out of hand. The new governess is inexperienced and lacks firmness! But you have not told us where Nanny Mackintosh is this afternoon. I have brought her the knitting pattern she was admiring."

"Nanny has gone to Edinburgh for a few days, Nanny Pritchard." I remember Nanny Mackintosh telling me never to impart matters of a personal nature to anyone. I decide to make my excuses and leave.

"I must take the girls home now. Miss Alexandra is rolling in the snow like a puppy and will catch cold. Come along, girls." Miss Portia obeys at once, but her sister does not want to leave the park.

"No, no, no!" she shouts, defiantly.

A tantrum is in the air, and the nannies will no doubt report to Nanny Mackintosh on her return that, like the young governess, I lack firmness.

"Yes, yes, yes, Miss Alexandra!" I say. I pick up the little girl, put her in her carriage, and we walk home under snow-laden skies.

A fire burns brightly in the nursery hearth. Soon it will be dark and time to turn on the lamps. I love this brief time before tea, with only the firelight making shadows on the whitewashed walls. I teach the girls how to make shadow shapes, how to hold their hands and transform them into birds, flying across the wall.

Suddenly the door of Nanny's room opens. *She cannot possibly have returned already?*

"Back, are you? Having a nice rest by the fire?" It is Roberts. Her face wears its customary sneer as she swings her bucket to and fro, the cloth draped over the side.

"What were you doing in Nanny Mackintosh's room?" I ask. No one is permitted in Nanny's room unless she is present.

"What do you think I'm doing? Not that it's any of your concern. I'm taking a look round to see if the room needs a good turnout while Nanny Mackintosh is away. That's what Mrs. Ransom said I was to do. I've done it and now I'm off. I've no time to sit and play pretty games," she says and brushes past me. *Roberts must have been spying on us!*

She pretends to lose her balance, and some of the water spills on the floor.

"Oh dear, look what I've gone and done." She bends down, peering exaggeratedly at the spilled water. Something clatters onto the linoleum. It is a small spoon with delicate markings. I manage to pick it up before she does. I recognize the spoon, for I was present when Nanny showed it to Miss Portia. I overheard her say it had been a gift from her grandmother in Scotland.

"I'll put the spoon back where it belongs, Roberts. Nanny Mackintosh likes to polish that herself. Please clean up the spill before you leave the nursery."

"I'll not take orders from a chit of a girl like you!" Roberts says.

"I am in charge while Nanny Mackintosh is away!" I say.

Roberts picks up the pail and empties the remaining water on the floor. "Then take charge and clean up the mess! I'm not doing it no more. You're like a silly sheep–*baa, baa*–following that nanny around. You'll turn out just like her, a bitter old maid. Serve you right." She pulls my cap off and drops it in the puddle. "And don't you even think about telling tales to Mr. Briggs or Mrs. Ransom! It was you who caused me to spill the water. Anyone can have an accident. As for Nanny's spoon, it's tarnished. All I was doing was taking it downstairs to shine it up!" Roberts hisses like a witch in a children's story. "Get out of my way," she says, and gives me a push.

"Don't you dare threaten me. Get out, and don't come back to the nursery until you can tell the truth," I say, opening the door wide. She does go, and I hear her clatter down the stairs. I wish I had given her a good slap. Then I remember the children!

I turn around. Miss Portia is wide-eyed, staring horrified at the mess, her hands over her ears. Miss Alexandra cries and cries, and I long to do the same. Instead, I pick up my soiled cap and throw it into the hamper to rinse out later. I must first get the girls to calm down. I lift Miss Alexandra up, sit her on my knee, and wipe her tears away with the corner of my apron.

"Who wants to help me clean up the mess?"

"Me! Me!" In seconds, the girls are on their knees getting their pinafores soaking wet while I rush to fetch old rags. When all is dry again and I have changed their pinafores and found myself a clean cap, we sit by the fire. I do my best to smooth over what just took place. *What set Roberts off?* I wonder. *Surely she would not be stupid enough to steal a spoon? Is she trying to get me dismissed?*

"Sometimes Master Harold plays roughly with his sister," I tell the girls. "Don't you and Master Roger disagree sometimes? It is soon over, Miss Portia, once everyone says they are sorry."

"I don't like Roberts. Send her away, Gardy," Miss Portia says. I wish I *could* send her away....

"I am sure Roberts is sorry for what she did, just as I am for speaking so harshly to her. I shall tell her so. Nanny would say, 'Roberts and Gardener do not deserve any cake for tea!' But you have been very good girls and you shall have cake. Look how nice and shiny you have made our floor. And now, let us forget all about it."

When Charlie Phipps brings up our tea a few minutes later, no one would guess that anything untoward had happened. "Enjoy your tea, young ladies," he says, and the little girls giggle. He is such a nice young man.

That evening, it is Croft who brings up my cocoa and biscuits. She's always friendly, with a smile for everyone, though being Mrs. Porter's kitchen maid can't be a bed of roses in a busy household. If it had been Roberts, the cocoa would have been slopped in the saucer....

"Thank you, Croft. Can you stay a bit? I miss not going down to the servants' hall."

"I can stay only a minute. Mrs. Porter's fit to be tied—a venison pie she baked for tomorrow's lunch is missing. The foreign secretary is to dine with Lord Milton. If that were not enough, Mr. Briggs says the silver is short. Three silver spoons have disappeared since he counted them after breakfast!"

"Do they suspect one of us?" I ask, wondering whether I should tell Croft about Roberts.

"They think they know. Roberts was supposed to be in by nine o'clock. It's her evening off, but she's always late coming back. Mrs. Ransom has had to warn her twice. Roberts is walking out with some fly-by-night, a fellow who works down at the race-track. Seeing as Roberts and I share a room, I am the one she confides in. I believe she has run off with him. When Mrs. Ransom and Mr. Briggs and I came downstairs to check our room, we saw at a glance that Roberts' clothes and boxes were gone. She's been planning it for a while, I shouldn't wonder. They think she had time to slip away this afternoon, when the kitchen was empty.

"I think he lost money on the horses and made her steal whatever she could for him to sell. Roberts hasn't liked it here since Nanny refused to consider her for the position of nursemaid. I'm not sorry to see the back of her, and that's the truth!

"I'll have to go. Mrs. Porter is in a bad mood, needing to bake another pie. She'll be waiting for me to help her, and there's the servants' hall to tidy. We're shorthanded now that Roberts has gone."

Two days later, a new scullery maid appears. She's thin as a wraith and hasn't lifted her eyes to look at anyone yet. Dean says she's from the orphanage.

She knocks at the door of the nursery as if I were a proper nanny. She scrubs the floor and polishes the brass fender around the fireplace as if her life depends on it. I'll never live up to her high standards and I tell her so! Her name is Good. I can imagine the teasing she gets with a name like that! *Good Riddance, Good Looking, Good Gracious*, poor thing. No wonder she's shy!

Next time she comes up to clean, I tell her, "This is my first place too, but everyone is nice. You'll see." She manages a smile and a whispered thanks.

No one knows if Lord Milton sent for the police, but Croft overheard Mrs. Porter tell Mr. Briggs, "Mark my words, Mr. Briggs, Roberts will come to a bad end, and no mistake! Who is going to employ her without a character? I never did take to her and that's the truth!"

9

An Accident

"**N**anny's back," Dean whispers, when we return from our afternoon walk. I'm glad I did not stay out any longer—Nanny will be glancing impatiently at the nursery clock! Miss Alexandra walks much of the way home on most days, but the March wind is sharp today, and it was too cold for us to wait while she inspected every leaf and paving stone.

"I am very sorry about your loss, Nanny Mackintosh," I say, on entering the nursery. "The children have missed you."

"Thank you, Gardener." I expect her to say something more, but she turns away. When Good comes in to clear the tea things, Nanny asks her name. The new girl is so nervous that she drops a knife. Flushing scarlet, she picks it up with a mumbled apology and says, "Good, ma'am."

She is scarcely out of the door before Nanny offers her opinion. "What an unfortunate name for someone so clumsy! Change the children's frocks please, Gardener. It will not do to keep Lord and Lady Milton waiting on my first day back."

I had hoped that Nanny would return softened, or at least a little more approachable. But no pleasant words are exchanged between us, however hard I try to please her. And Miss Portia has found herself banished to the corner twice in two days, for some trifling fault.

I am happy to return to the servants' hall after spending my evenings alone, upstairs, while Nanny has been away. I thought she'd be going down to Mrs. Ransom's parlor, but she complains of a migraine.

Hart is with us tonight. More often, she accompanies Lord and Lady Milton to the opera or a dinner party, but this evening she sits beside Mr. Harris, who is most attentive to her. She takes no more notice of him than of anyone else, but I find him most pleasant and nice-looking, too! Hart works hard, waiting up for her ladyship to come home, taking care of her beautiful gowns, and arranging her hair in becoming styles. She is the one who brings Lady Milton her early-morning tea, no matter how late she has waited up the night before. Dean says Hart keeps the bedroom and dressing rooms to perfection. And Hart is a good needle-woman as well.

Mrs. Porter offers us wedges of savory pie. There has been a fork supper earlier for twenty guests, so we are to enjoy the leftover treat. After she gives me a slice to take up to Nanny, she takes me by surprise: "You will miss her and the children when they sail to New York, Gardener!"

I am bewildered. *Sail to New York?* Nanny has not mentioned a word about it to me, nor has anyone else!

"Hadn't you heard, Gardener?" Dean says. "Lord and Lady Milton are sailing on the maiden voyage of the *Titanic* and will take the girls. Lady Milton's sister is Miss Alexandra's godmother and has not seen her since the christening. You'll be sharing a cabin with Nanny Mackintosh, won't you, Hart?"

"Yes, and I shall have my hands full. The *Titanic* is the most luxurious liner ever built. I've been informed that Lady Milton will have to be dressed even more fittingly than usual. It means changes of outfits and restyling her hair two or three times a day! New gowns have been ordered from *Maison Lucile* in Hanover Square, designs imported from the Paris salon. We will spend six days at sea, a week in New York, and another week coming back. I'll have six or seven trunks to pack, at the very least!"

"You and Nanny will be waited on hand and foot," Mrs. Porter says.

Charlie Phipps winks at me. "That will be nothing new for Nanny Mackintosh–isn't that so, Gardener?"

I take no notice of him, knowing that Mr. Briggs won't tolerate any criticism from the staff about our employers or each other. "That will do, Phipps," he says.

"Don't you wish you were going on the *Titanic* too, Gardener?" Phipps asks me.

"No, thanks. I cannot swim, and the very idea of sailing so far away, with nothing to look at but the ocean, makes me shudder!" The moment I answer him, I wish I hadn't spoken so freely.

Phipps leans back and laughs and laughs before Mr. Briggs gives him a sharp look, and he stops. Nevertheless, my evening is spoiled.

The first time I heard the name *Titanic* was last Christmas. We had all gone over to Uncle Alf's house. He was giving a party for family, friends, and neighbors. There was a young man, Patrick O'Connor, over from Belfast for the holidays. He's the nephew of one of the porters at the market, who helps out at the stall now and then. Patrick could not take his eyes from Kathleen. Later she told me he'd said that he's eighteen and has been working on the *Titanic,* helping to install boilers.

———

"Have you ever been to sea, Mr. Briggs?" Mr. Harris asks him.

"No, but my brother-in-law is a steward in first class on the *Olympic*, *Titanic*'s sister ship. He does the Atlantic run to New York and was on the maiden voyage last year. My brother-in-law says the *Titanic* is even grander than his own ship. There is a swimming bath, a Turkish bath, and a fully equipped gymnasium, as well as a squash court. Imagine, some of the first-class parlor suites even have private promenades." The drawing room bell rings, and Mr. Briggs pushes his chair back, saying, "On your feet, Phipps. Time to bring in the sherry."

Mrs. Porter asks, "Where is Nanny Mackintosh's cocoa, Croft?" I take the tray Croft hands me, wondering what my duties will be when everyone in the nursery is away. I'd happily scrub and scour every room in the house—and there are some I have never been inside—rather than go on a sea voyage. I cannot imagine what it would be like to be surrounded by so much water! I worry about Miss Alexandra, in particular. She can be willful and needs more than one pair of eyes to stop her running off in search of adventures. *Suppose she falls overboard?* I have never seen Nanny Mackintosh vary her slow, deliberate gait....

Next day, Mrs. Ransom puts up the servants' schedule. The nurseries are to be whitewashed and papered from April 11–15, then Good and I will spring-clean after the workmen have left. The holiday list is up too—mine is from April 20–27. I wasn't expecting a week until the end of my first year in June, but as the family is away, I suppose that is a convenient time. *Won't Mother and Emily be happy?* Kath and I have managed to meet only twice on my evenings off lately, so she'll be excited at my being home too. I'll no doubt be hearing more about Patrick O'Connor. On our last walk, she did not stop talking about him the whole time!

"Lou, Patrick says his feelings for me are serious, and I like him too. He writes to me at the salon. He'll be going on the one-day sea trial for the *Titanic*, setting off from Belfast on April 2nd to make sure the ship is ready for the maiden voyage. He's been taken on as stoker and hopes the crew will get shore leave before they sail to America. If he does, he plans to come to London and spend the day with me!

"After he returns from America, he is going to ask Father's permission for us to walk out together. He doesn't think it right that we meet in secret! In some ways, he is quite old-fashioned, almost as bad as Father. Oh, Lou, don't you think Patrick is awfully handsome?"

"But, Kathleen, you would never marry a sailor, would you? You'd hardly ever see him, and what about all your dreams of having a career and the salon?" She is not much older than me!

"I can do both, can't I? This is 1912; the world is not like it used to be. We can do anything we want. When I marry Patrick, you will be my bridesmaid, and I shall make you the most wonderful hat in London. It's all ahead of us, Lou–the whole world!"

"There will be nothing at all ahead for me if I'm late getting back. I'm happy for you, Kath, but don't be in too much of a hurry, will you?"

On the morning of Friday, April 5, Nanny is getting ready for her day off. I have just finished sorting out the toy box and have set aside a few toys for the children to take on the voyage. I am still sitting on the floor, and Miss Alexandra and Miss Portia clamber over me, squabbling over a teddy bear. I take no notice until Nanny comes out of her room, glaring at us. She claps her hands, startling the children.

"Really, Gardener, sometimes I despair of you ever remembering your place! Girls, go and sit at the table in silence and fold your hands. Gardener, it is almost time for your walk. Take the nursery umbrella; it looks like rain. I am about to leave."

"Yes, Nanny, have a pleasant day." *It is so much nicer in the nursery when she is not here!*

Nanny Mackintosh sails out dressed in black. She will be in mourning for a year, on account of her father. I notice the hem of her black skirt is longer than the customary uniform she wears.

Suddenly I hear a cry and a thud, as if a box or trunk has been dropped. I did not see Nanny carrying anything other than her umbrella and rush out to see what has happened. To my dismay, Nanny Mackintosh lies crumpled at the bottom of the stairs. I close the gate at the top and run down to her. Nanny's face is white, one leg is bent unnaturally beneath her, and she holds her arm, moaning in pain.

"Don't try to move, Nanny, I'm going for help!" Luckily, Dean is downstairs, dusting. She calls Mrs. Ransom. Mr. Briggs and Phipps arrive moments later, and Mrs. Ransom tells them to carry Nanny into her own parlor and to inform Lady Milton. No doubt the doctor will be sent for.

"Did you see what happened, Gardener?"

"No, Mrs. Ransom. I heard Nanny fall and came to see if I could help."

"Nanny Mackintosh will be looked after. Return to your duties, please," she says.

I go back up, reluctantly, wishing I could stay to find out what the doctor says. This mishap will not improve Nanny's temper, I'm afraid. I hope she is not in too great discomfort.

As soon as we reach the park, the nannies ask me to sit down, curious to find out why Nanny Mackintosh is not here to learn about Nanny Gilbert's new knitting stitch. They manage to pry the story of the accident out of me. Their conjectures, sympathy, advice, and tut-tutting last until a spring shower sends us all on our way.

Dean is waiting. She says I am wanted in the drawing room and she will take the girls back upstairs. "I hope Lady Milton won't keep you long, Gardener. Mrs. Porter is in a state, all behind with her dinner. Croft and I are trying to be in three places at once, what with the doctor requiring tea, prescriptions to be collected, and a bed to be made up for Nanny downstairs." I hurry away, patting my hair in place as I go.

"You wish to see me, Lady Milton?" I ask, as I enter the room. Mrs. Ransom stands next to her ladyship, and both look gravely at me. I can't think what I may have done wrong!

Lady Milton says, "You will be sorry to hear that Nanny Mackintosh has broken both her wrist and her ankle. She will be unable to use the stairs for some time and will be staying downstairs with Mrs. Ransom. As we sail in five days, this comes at a most inconvenient time. I am reluctant to hire anyone new to take Nanny's place at such short notice." She looks at Mrs. Ransom for confirmation, and the housekeeper murmurs something to Lady Milton, who nods. I wait, growing more nervous by the second.

"The children are accustomed to you, Gardener. You have made an excellent impression both on my husband and my mother...and so, despite your youth, we have decided that you will accompany us in Nanny's stead."

I am too shocked and horrified to manage more than a few stuttered words. "But, ma'am, I mean, Lady Milton..." *How can I explain that I would do anything for the children, except to go on an ocean voyage?* "Please don't make me go!" I try to speak the words, but they go unheeded, unheard. *Did I actually voice them?*

"Very well, Gardener, I will leave the details for Mrs. Ransom to explain." She sweeps out, and I just have enough presence of mind to remember to open the door for her.

"I hope you appreciate what an exceptional opportunity you have been offered, Gardener. You will be the envy of the servants' hall," the housekeeper says.

I would welcome any one of them to go instead of me. *I must try and explain to Mrs. Ransom before it is too late!*

"Please, Mrs. Ransom, I would much prefer to stay and spring-clean the nurseries."

"That will do, Gardener. Your preferences are of no consequence. You have my permission to take tomorrow afternoon and evening off to see your family. You will return at nine o'clock, as usual. Your annual holiday will be postponed.

"I am informed by her ladyship that you will share a suite with Hart and the young ladies. Nanny Mackintosh's misfortune has placed you in a position beyond anything a girl of your station and age could ever hope for. No wonder you are tongue-tied. Let us hope you do not let us down! That will be all for the present; you may go."

I do not sleep a wink the whole night. *If only I can find a way out!* I almost wish I had the courage to run away. *Could I tell Mother and Father that I want to stay home after all?*

10

Saying Good-bye

When I arrive home next day, Mother takes one look at my face and sends Emily upstairs to play with George. She pours us both cups of tea and sits down facing me.

"It is not your day off and I can see you are upset. There's no need to be afraid, Lou. Tell me the truth, and I'll stand by you if you're in some kind of trouble. Have they dismissed you? Without a character reference, is that it?" I can't help it, my eyes fill with tears.

"If it was only that, Mother..." I take a deep breath, and my words pour out in a rush. "I am to go to America, to sail on the maiden voyage of the *Titanic*. Nanny Mackintosh has had an accident, and I'm to take her place. Mother, I can't–don't make me go!"

Mother understands, doesn't she? She must—nothing escapes her about any of us!

Mother lifts her tea to her lips, sips, and puts it down again. She wraps her hands around the mug as if to warm them. Then she looks up and our eyes meet. In that instant, I know she is thinking of another day, when no amount of tea could bring comfort. She does understand. I knew she would!

"If you can't go, it is only fair to let Lady Milton know at once, Lou, so that she may hire someone else. But is that what you really want? I thought you had settled down nicely. I'm sure there's no end of girls who would jump at the chance of taking your place. Are you going to come running home like this forever because of what happened? It was an accident, Lou. There isn't a day goes by that I'm not reminded of Johnny. I've had to get on with life; we all have. If I thought there was any danger, I'd do my best to stop you going so far away. But you'll be home safe and sound in less than a month. You have to make up your own mind, Louisa, I can't do it for you. Here's Father. Let's see what he thinks about your going."

My father walks into the kitchen. "Now that's a nice surprise. Not your day off, is it, Lou?" Mother tells him about the maiden voyage. I've a lump in my throat.

"Upon my word, they must think a lot of you! Going to America, where the streets are paved with gold; and on the finest, safest ship ever to come out of Belfast? Aren't you a lucky girl!" Father beams at me, his face shining with pride.

All at once, I make my decision. I have been given an opportunity to go farther than anyone in our family has ever been and to the other side of the world. *Isn't that what I always dreamed of doing? To see what's out there? To discover what I can do and be? Me, Louisa Gardener, the one in the middle, who thought she'd never get her chance?* I've got to stop being so scared of everything new that comes my way!

"Very well, I'll go," I say.

"Of course you will. Isn't that what you came home to tell us? Or were you planning to tell her ladyship that the idea is not to your liking?" If only Father knew how close he is to the truth! He chuckles, as if at some great joke. Mother doesn't join in. Her rough, work-worn hand covers mine.

"It's natural to feel a bit nervous, Lou. And you, too, Flo," Father says. "But that ship is a wonder. Close to a thousand feet she is, big enough to hold over three thousand people. They say she is a floating lifeboat, she's that safe! Over three thousand rivets holding her together. I should know; aren't I down at the docks every week? And the food that is going on board–thirty-six thousand oranges and seven thousand heads of lettuce, Flo!" Father carries on as if he were supplying the food personally.

When Kathleen comes home, the story has to be told all over again. After supper, Father suggests that Kathleen walk part of the way back with me.

"Good-bye, my girl, mind you keep safe and sound," he says, and Mother kisses my cheek. She smiles so lovingly that I almost change my mind about going! As Kathleen and I walk away from the house, I look back and Mother is standing outside the door, watching us. She waves for a long time.

"I know what you are thinking, Lou," Kathleen says, "but it is not going to be like those nightmares you used to have. The little girls will not fall into the water, and no one will drown, least of all you! Patrick says this ship is unsinkable. He'd not be down in the boiler room shoveling coal into the furnaces if there was any danger. He wants to come home safely, back to me!"

She unbuttons her coat, takes it off, and holds it out. "This will keep you warm. April evenings can get cold. Go on, Lou, take it."

"No, thanks, Kath, this is your new spring coat. You saved up so long for it!"

"It's a loan—you'll bring it back looking as good as new, I am sure. I want to think of my little sister strolling on the deck in the moonlight...sailing on the same ship as Patrick and wearing my new spring coat."

"And suppose there is no moon?"

"No moon? There is always a moon. I wish I was

going with you!"

"So do I. And thanks, Kath, I'll be proud to borrow your coat." I hang it carefully over my arm. My sister shivers and squeezes my arm before she hurries home, away from me.

I'm worn out from running up and down stairs, summoned by Nanny, to listen to endless instructions, reproofs, and warnings! With every word, she makes clear how much she disapproves of my youth, my inexperience, and the imprudence of letting me take her place on the voyage.

If Nanny does not permit me to finish all I've yet to do, I have a mind to suggest that she let Phipps carry her back upstairs, so that she may personally fold each garment with her one good hand. And if I'm becoming waspish, it is her fault! Nanny means well, believing it her duty to instruct me, so I try to hide my impatience. Lady Milton has taken the children out, accompanied by Hart, to purchase new shoes for Miss Portia and Miss Alexandra. I had hoped to finish the ironing while they were absent.

Nanny goes on and on: "Routine, Gardener, establish your routine the moment you get on board ship, to the best of your ability." Her lips tighten. "When you reach New York, discipline must be maintained. I have it on good authority that Americans are far more lax with their children than we are. We must

uphold our standards as best we can, trying circumstances or not.

"Lady Milton has arranged for you and the children
to partake of your meals in your stateroom on board
ship—a most appropriate decision. Let us hope the
chef will see the children are not given rich food. I
do not wish to have to deal with overindulged and
spoiled girls on your return."

Nanny lowers her voice as though fearing to be
overheard. "I shall have my hands full as it is, what
with another baby due later this year."

I know better than to comment, but I had sus-
pected from one or two remarks that I'd overheard
Mrs. Porter smilingly make to Hart about untouched
breakfast trays! I remember how Mother could never
face anything more than a biscuit and a cup of tea
before noon, when George was on the way.

"Yes, Nanny," I say and turn to leave, hoping she's
finished. I've a dozen tasks waiting for me to do.

"One more thing, Gardener—remember your place!"
*Now why does she think she has to tell me that? Does
she think I am going to run off with a sailor?* "Passengers
on board ship are inclined to be rather too friendly
and sometimes do not make sufficient distinctions
between...what I am endeavoring to say is, you are a
servant. Conduct yourself accordingly and discour-
age familiarity of any kind!"

"I shall be far too occupied, Nanny Mackintosh,

making sure that Miss Alexandra does not try to climb over the ship's railings, to have time to encourage any familiarity." And this time I do go upstairs. One can only remain meek and silent so long!

On Tuesday morning, our last day before we are to leave, I go down to collect new cream-colored sailor frocks from Mrs. Wilson. She holds up the perfect small garments to show me before carefully draping them over my arm.

"I don't hold with maiden voyages, myself. You would never catch me leaving dry land!"

I don't reply, not having had a say in the matter and wishing only that I were not subjected to everyone's opinions and warnings about the voyage. Lord Milton dotes on her ladyship and worships his daughters. He would never put them into danger.

"The dresses are beautiful, Mrs. Wilson. However did you manage all those pleats? Thank you very much for getting them finished in time," I say.

"Turn round, Gardener. Those hems will need lengthening when you get back. It won't take me a minute on the machine, not like the old days when we did everything by hand. It doesn't do to show too much ankle." She looks at me sharply.

What is the matter with everyone? It must be Spring putting ideas into everyone's head. No one is going to take any notice of me.

Croft pokes her head around the door. "I've made you a nice bacon sandwich, Mrs. Wilson. Mrs. Porter says not to let it get cold and would you come into the servants' hall, if you please." She holds the door open for the old woman and motions me to wait.

"I've got something for you, Gardener," Croft whispers. She hands me an envelope from her apron pocket. "I found it this morning, pushed under the back door. Got a young man writing to you, have you? I don't know what a certain Mr. Phipps would say to that!" she says.

"Mr. Phipps? Whatever gave you that idea? And when would I have any time for a young man?" I say, knowing she's only teasing me. "This is my sister's handwriting. But thanks, Croft. I've got to go and finish my packing." I hurry back upstairs.

Kathleen must have got up very early to get this to me before going to work. I glance at it quickly.

Dear Lou,

Please give the enclosed to Patrick when you get on board ship. Try to keep an eye on him. I don't trust all those rich ladies! Thanks.

Your loving sister,
Kathleen

I do not mean to pry, but I can't help seeing the few words written on the back of one of *Madame Claudine*'s cards: *I will be waiting for you when you come back in a fortnight's time. Fondly, Kathleen.*

How hard can it be to find a member of the crew called *Patrick O' Connor*? I shall give him Kathleen's note as soon as I am able. That's the least I can do, when she was generous enough to lend me her smart new coat!

It seems I have hardly put my head down on the pillow when it is time to get up. The great dreaded day–Wednesday, April 10–has arrived!

I dress the sleepy children, coax them to eat a very early breakfast, and bundle them into their warm coats. Mr. Harris waits by the Daimler, ready to drive us all to Southampton, where we are to board the ship. The luggage was carried down last night. Lord Milton wishes to arrive at the dock before the arrival of the boat train, bringing most of the second- and third-class passengers. Croft helps Dean to stow the picnic hamper away. The household staff–all except for Nanny–waits outside to bid us bon voyage. Lady Milton is the last one to come down. Hart carries her furs and yet another hatbox.

I try to enjoy the beautiful spring countryside that greets us as we leave London behind. But not even the comfort of the dark blue leather upholstery nor the excitement of the journey is sufficient for me to overcome my feeling of dread.

"It's to test you, Lou," Kath said. *What kind of test?* That's what I'd like to know. Everyone made anxious—Lady Milton, Nanny Mackintosh—and for what?

I am fourteen years old, not a five-year-old making sand castles and losing myself in playing with seashells. As long as I have sufficient breath in my body, Miss Portia and Miss Alexandra will come to no harm!

I'll get to know every inch of the ship, every nook and corner, and teach Miss Alexandra and Miss Portia to stop where they are if we should ever get separated. That way, I'll be able to find them should they ever get lost, though I can't think how that would happen as they are never left unattended! I'll make sure that the girls are as safe and happy as if we were in our own nurseries at home...happier, because I am not going to find fault with them the second they look as if they are enjoying themselves. I am determined that this will be my last mean thought about poor Nanny Mackintosh.

Southampton, England

1912

II

Titanic

We have arrived. Mr. Harris opens the door for us to alight. And there is the ship, about which I have heard so much! It is as tall as a mountain, with its shining black hull and its long white decks–rising higher and higher, like the tiers on a wedding cake–looming up against the sky. Then, higher still, so that I must crane my neck to see the top, four tall black funnels. *How did they ever build anything so large? And how can something so huge sail across the ocean in only one week?* I think of Patrick shoveling coal, helping the vessel to reach America.

I am dazzled at the sight of the *Titanic*. The great crowd of people, gazing up from the dockside, seem as much in awe as I am, all of us dwarfed by the vast ship. I never imagined it would be so overwhelming.

The wonder and the mystery frighten me, more so when I realize we are embarking on the ship's maiden voyage.

The children, impatient to board, tug at my hands. We follow their parents, past the third- and second-class gangways to our first-class one, up and onto the ship. A white uniformed officer stands at the top. He checks his lordship's boarding pass, hands it back, and says, "Welcome to the *Titanic*." He points out the lift that will carry us up to our deck. I have never been inside a lift before. Lord Milton requests B deck, a button is pressed, and miraculously we are carried up.

The smartly uniformed lift boy, who does not look a day older than fifteen, informs us, "Captain Smith has given permission for second-class passengers to explore the ship before sailing." He goes on to reassure Lady Milton and the other occupants of the lift: "Once we get underway, all classes will return to their own quarters, and it will be nice and quiet. We pick up our last passengers at Cherbourg today and from Queenstown tomorrow. In all, there will be three hundred first-class passengers aboard!" The lift stops, the door glides open as if by magic, and the children are as enchanted as I am by the smooth ride.

"Again, Papa, please," Miss Alexandra says, but Lord Milton picks her up and carries her out of the lift and along a carpeted corridor to a door marked 70-72.

"These are the staterooms reserved for Hart, Gardener, and the girls," Lady Milton says. "My husband and I are nearby, in parlor suite 74-76. Hart will fetch you and the children presently, Gardener, to join us on deck to watch the departure of the ship."

Hart, still carrying the hatbox, follows her and Lord Milton into their suite, further along the corridor.

I open our door, and the children and I go inside. *Can this really be for us?* The bedroom doors are open in welcome, and the luggage is already waiting for me to unpack. A beautifully arranged bouquet of flowers stands beside a basket of fruit on the round table in the sitting area. Everything looks brand-new, as though someone has just a moment ago placed it there. I must keep reminding myself that it *is* brand-new and that we are the first passengers to sail on the *Titanic*.

I almost expect to leave a fingerprint when I touch something. Compared to their plain nurseries at home, with furnishings chosen for children's spills and sturdy wear, it looks like a palace. The girls wriggle and squeal with impatience to explore their new home.

"We must not touch any of these beautiful things until our hands are spotless. You never know if the captain will hold an inspection," I say, doing my best

to look serious. I lead the way into a luxurious bathroom, with a large deep bathtub and a marble wash-
stand. On the shelf below the mirror is an electric
curling iron. I had expected a simple washbasin
and jug, not these shining brass taps marked hot
and cold, gushing out clear water the moment I
turn them on! I roll up my sleeves and half-fill the
basin. When I test that the water is the right temperature, I pick up a cake of soap. It is wrapped in
paper embossed with a picture of the *Titanic* sailing
through the waves. I shall save the wrapping of the
fragrant-smelling Vinolia soap as a souvenir. For
once, my charges endure being washed without
complaint and dry their own faces and hands on
the soft white towels.

I have never slept in a room with a carpet, or
indeed in a new bed made up with brand-new linen.
The room that Hart and I are to share has two brass
beds, covered with lace bedspreads. We have two
bedside tables as well as a marble-topped dressing
table and a roomy wardrobe.

The girls have discovered their own bedroom and
bounce up and down on the large brass bed.

"My sister Kathleen and I always share a bed at
home," I say. "It is much smaller than this lovely
one." The girls look at each other, and I notice a glint
of mischief. Well, it won't be the first time I have
taken part in or had to stop a pillow fight!

Mr. Briggs has said that windows are called port-holes aboard ship. I imagined they would be small and round, not at all like these, which are larger than our nursery ones and elegantly curtained in pink. I shall have so much to tell them at home when I return! There are pink-shaded lamps, an electric fire, a ceiling fan, a writing desk in one corner, and a small blue sofa with matching armchairs in the parlor.

I decide to unpack after lunch, when the girls have a nap. I would truly prefer to stay and do it now than go out on deck. If I had not looked out of the port-hole, I could convince myself that we are not on the water at all!

"This is beautiful," Hart says, as she comes in. She takes a quick admiring look around. "Everyone is exclaiming about the elegance of the staterooms, our steward said. I had to ring for more vases because Lord and Lady Milton have been sent so many bou-quets! Did you know, Gardener, that this voyage is to celebrate their tenth wedding anniversary?

"You are to bring the children, now, please, to join their parents on the first-class promenade, on A deck. The warning whistle, for visitors to leave the ship, has been sounded twice. I'll be staying below to arrange Lady Milton's things. I can watch the *Titanic*'s departure from one of our windows."

The girls are delighted to go up in the lift again. We walk along smooth teak decks, past a glass-walled reading room. A glance in reveals deep leather chairs grouped around a fire. Further along the deck is the partly sheltered Verandah Café and Palm Court, where Lady Milton converses with another lady.

Miss Portia and Miss Alexandra immediately hop from one white square to a black one on the check-ered floor. The white wicker furniture and ivy trail-ing along the walls remind me of the gazebo in Lady Portman's garden. It is hard to believe how all this is possible on board a ship!

"There you are, Gardener. Portia, Alexandra, come and say good afternoon. Mrs. Spedden has a little boy, Robert, who is your age. You may play with him tomorrow afternoon, Portia. Gardener will bring you here, after your rest. Mrs. Spedden tells me that French vanilla ice cream will be served at tea."

Miss Portia's eyes sparkle. The spoiling has begun, and I am thankful Nanny Mackintosh is not here to comment.

"Come along, my dear, the ship is about to sail." Lord Milton bows to the ladies, offers his arm to his wife, and I follow along with the girls to the open part of the deck. I envy Hart, whose duties keep her inside, and try not to look down at the water. A breeze ruffles my cap, and I am glad of Kathleen's coat. Lord and

Lady Milton greet several of the other passengers.

"Andrews, my dear fellow," Lord Milton addresses a gentleman who is absorbed in some detail of the lounge entrance. "The *Titanic* is more than you promised–a triumph of design. My congratulations!" Lord Milton shakes hands with the gentleman.

"Indeed, Mr. Andrews, how gratified you must be to see the fruits of all your hard work," Lady Milton says. "It is hard to believe that this is a maiden voyage. I have not come across a single item that can be improved upon. I told Rupert I have quite made up my mind to change the decor of my sitting room in London to match the beautiful Italian Renaissance decor in our suite."

"I can see that I will have much to answer for to the gentlemen on board if all the ladies demand new furnishings, Lady Milton. However, I still have to decide on final colors of the wicker furniture on the starboard side. More hooks are required in the suites," Mr. Andrews says.

"Nevertheless, I do hope that you will find time to join us for dinner in the à la carte restaurant, tomorrow perhaps? Lord and Lady Duff Gordon will be in our party. Do say you will come." Lady Milton smiles at the gentleman.

"I shall be delighted, ma'am. Until tomorrow, then." Mr. Andrews bows and is immediately absorbed again in his inspection of the ship.

"Well done, my dear. Andrews never stops working. I shall have to persuade him to join me in a game of squash, or a visit to the gymnasium. Come along, everyone."

I stand close behind the girls and their parents at the railings, ready, if needed, to remove the children. We are so high up on the deck, only one below the boat deck, how small we must appear to the people waving on the quay below.

"Look at the big wave, Papa." Miss Portia points to sprays of foam as the *Titanic* parts the water, churning it up as she starts her engines.

Lord Milton explains that our ship is going to turn into the River Test. He points to two smaller vessels that the *Titanic* must pass—the *New York* and the *Oceanic*, which are moored nearby.

Suddenly, there are a series of loud bangs, almost like shots. I hold the girls' hands tightly.

Lord Milton does not seem to be disturbed, however. "The *Titanic* has caused such a swell of water that the ropes holding the *New York* are unable to take the strain."

It is all I can do to hold myself back from running with the girls to the safety of our staterooms!

Lady Milton places her gloved hand on her husband's arm. "Rupert, the *New York* seems to be swinging towards us. There will surely be a collision!" she declares.

Why did I ever agree to come on this ship? We have barely left shore, and here we are in difficulties!

"Nonsense, Helen, my dear, you look quite pale. There is absolutely nothing for you to be concerned about. The tugs are on their way and will pull her back. Do you see them?"

Lord Milton lifts Miss Alexandra up into his arms.

"Look at the little tugboats, Alexandra! My word, your big brother would enjoy this. I shall write to him this afternoon and tell him all about our adventure."

"*Toot, toot.*" The little girl imitates the sound of the tugs, adding her voice to the buzz of excitement from the other passengers, who are leaning over the railings. I shudder to watch them.

"There now, my dear, Captain Smith has reversed the ship. We are traveling backwards in perfect safety. I have the utmost confidence in him. After all, this is his final voyage after thirty years' service at sea. I'd trust him with every life on board. Nevertheless, I admit that was a close shave!" Lord Milton tells his wife.

A close shave? What little confidence I have managed to muster seeps away. *How will I ever survive the next week?* Not only that, we have to sail back again!

"Down now, please, Papa." Miss Alexandra wriggles in her father's arms, and he hands her to me. I grasp her arm, firmly, before she can run off among the other spectators, or attempt to climb up on one of the railings.

A family stands nearby, the nanny holding a baby boy in her arms. A little girl of perhaps two fidgets between her parents. No doubt, this child has captured Miss Alexandra's attention. The nanny looks familiar...*perhaps I have seen her walking in the park?* She seems to notice my stare, turns, and looks down. Now I know who she reminds me of: Roberts! It cannot be her. She could not obtain a position without a reference. And this person's hair is deep red under her cap!

A bugle sounds, loud enough for Miss Portia to run to me and hold my hand. *What now?* Lord Milton looks delighted. The bugle plays "The Roast Beef of Old England."

"Ah, lunch at last!" he says. "We are on our way, an hour late—it is already one o'clock. However, we will soon make up the time. The purser mentioned some of the male passengers are already placing bets on the ship reaching New York at least a day ahead of schedule."

Seagulls scream high above us as we head back down to our own deck. Hart must have heard the bugle, for she waits at the door of the suite in readiness for Lord and Lady Milton's return.

"I shall be only ten minutes, Rupert. My hair is in

total disarray, Hart. Good-bye, my darlings, Mama and Papa will come and see you both this evening."

The ship is so steady, I am scarcely aware of the movement. In our own rooms, the table is laid daintily for lunch. Our luggage had been unpacked for us. *Are there elves aboard?*

No sooner are the girls washed and seated than there is a knock on the door and a stewardess enters, wheeling in our lunch. "Good afternoon, Miss Gardener, Miss Alexandra, and Miss Portia. I am Mrs. Landers, your stewardess. Chef was told simple fare, Miss Gardener. Should you have any special requests, please let me know." She sets the steaming dishes of fine blue-and-white china, edged with gold, on the table. Chef has sent up beef consommé, slices of roast beef and gravy, chicken lyonnaise, creamed carrots, duchess potatoes, minted peas, and freshly baked bread and butter. "Please ring for me when you have finished, and I will bring up your tea or coffee then."

"Tea, please, Mrs. Landers," I reply.

Miss Portia eyes the apple tart, fruit salad, and jugs of cream and custard on the trolley. "I was afraid there would be tapioca pudding. Ice cream is my favorite!" she confides.

I cannot believe our shy Miss Portia has spoken. *Has Nanny's absence helped her find her voice?* And I'm trying not to think unkindly about Nanny Mackintosh!

"I will mention your preference, Miss Portia." Mrs. Landers leaves us to enjoy a luncheon that would cause Nanny to launch into a lecture about digestion. *There I go again—it seems Nanny's influence has followed me right into our stateroom!*

After I have settled the girls down for their nap, I clear the table and put the dishes back on the trolley before I ring the bell. It seems strange ringing for someone to wait upon me; I feel uncomfortable about doing so. Mrs. Landers answers almost immediately, bringing a tray with tea, lemon, milk, and a dish of sugar cubes. I resolve to put a few away for the children as a treat.

"I hope everything was to your liking, Miss Gardener. Do tell me of anything else you require. And, Miss Gardener, it is part of my duties to serve and clear away. A nanny has enough to do, taking care of two little girls on board ship."

Is this what Nanny Mackintosh meant by knowing my place? I do not want to offend Mrs. Landers!

"I am not really the children's nanny, Mrs. Landers—I am their nursemaid. Their nanny had a fall just before the family was due to sail, and I was asked to take her place." I am surprised how difficult I find it to explain my position to the stewardess. Not because I am ashamed of being a nursemaid—it is a wonderful start for me, everyone says so—but...

"I am sure the children's parents are pleased that

their daughters have someone like you to take over, Miss Gardener," Mrs. Landers says. "There is a family on C deck returning to Canada with their staff: a nanny, cook, chauffeur, maid, and two very young children. I am told the nanny had to be hired at short notice, when the regular nanny took ill. In confidence, Miss Gardener, she seems ill at ease. I would have guessed that, unlike you, she is not used to handling such young charges." She pours out my tea.

Is she referring to the nanny who resembles Roberts? If it is her, I wonder if she is wearing a wig. Roberts always wanted to be a nursemaid, which caused the problem between us. I shall try to forget about her....

"Where are the life jackets kept, Mrs. Landers? Would you show me, please, how to fasten them, when it is convenient?"

"The life jackets are on top of the wardrobes. I will get them down for you this evening, after we have taken on more passengers in Cherbourg. Even after the last passengers come on board in Queenstown, Ireland, tomorrow, we will not be full. There have been a few cancellations. Some passengers are superstitious about embarking on a maiden voyage. But a vessel like this is built to weather any storms. Nothing can sink her, Miss Gardener. I have never seen an April with as calm an ocean and as mild a climate as this one! I am confident that you may look forward to a pleasant, carefree voyage on a happy ship. Our crew is a most experienced one.

"The bugle to dress is sounded one hour before meals. The first meal of the day is at seven o'clock, when tea, scones, and fruit are served for early risers. Breakfast is at eight o'clock. Lunch is at one, and the bugle to dress sounds again at six o'clock, for seven o'clock dinner. If it meets with your approval, I will serve dinner for you and the children at six o'clock."

"Thank you, Mrs. Landers. I did want to ask you something else: I have been wondering how you manage to get from one end of the ship to the other so quickly."

"We have an alleyway for the crew, running along the entire ship, on E deck. We call it Scotland Road. I wish you a pleasant afternoon, Miss Gardener."

The first chance I get tomorrow, I will find Scotland Road and Mr. Patrick O'Connor, who is sweet on my sister, and give him her note.

The Atlantic Ocean

1912

12

At Sea

I am as eager as the children to explore the ship. As soon as they wake up from their nap, we set off. We begin at the first-class entrance on the top deck, where the Grand Staircase begins. Miss Portia leads, her small pale fingers gripping the polished-wood railings. I follow behind, with Miss Alexandra. The stairs are covered in plush red carpet and wind down to the reception room on D deck. This opens out into the first-class dining room—the largest on the ship.

On each of the landings, all leading into elegant reception rooms, red velvet seats offer views of the scene below. We sit down in a cozy alcove.

"These stairs are where your mama and papa will descend tonight for dinner," I tell the girls. I try to imagine what it might be like if Kathleen and I were two of the splendidly dressed ladies on board, sitting here and whispering secrets, or gossiping behind our fans!

We continue our walk down to the next landing. The girls trail their fingers along the wrought-iron swirls of flowers and leaves ornamenting the balustrades beneath the railings.

Afternoon sunlight streams through the glass roof, making the crystal chandelier beneath glisten and glitter. Brass and gold surround us. I would like to spend the next hour or two admiring the elaborate paintings, which are hung all along the paneled walls. The little girls, however, are more fascinated by a great clock, which forms the centerpiece of a wooden panel. I pick up Miss Alexandra, so she may look more closely at the two carved figures holding the clock aloft. A gentleman nearby explains to his two lady companions that each carving represents Honor and Glory and the clock symbolizes Time.

We continue down, right to the bottom of the staircase. Here, all three of us are enchanted by a bronze sculpture of a baby cherub. He stands with wings outspread, holding a lamp. But Miss Alexandra has had enough of being good, and we make our way back to the lift. The door opens, and several passengers emerge, among them the nanny I had noticed earlier. She is turned away from us, but I can hear her admonishing the little girl in her care. She pulls the child's arm roughly.

"Not kind," Miss Portia whispers to me. "I don't like Roberts."

"This nanny is not Roberts," I reassure her. "Look at her red hair. Let's go back to our stateroom. Would you and Miss Alexandra like to draw a picture of the ship to send to your brother? I saw pencils and paper in the drawer of our little desk." They are happy to do so.

I am certain this was the temporary nanny Mrs. Landers mentioned to me earlier! *But isn't it odd that both Miss Portia and I noticed the resemblance to Roberts?*

When their parents come in to say good night, the little girls are too sleepy to protest about going to bed.

Lady Milton looks beautiful–Hart has dressed her so elegantly for the first evening's dinner. She wears a rope of pearls, drop pearl and amethyst earrings, and a tiara. Her gown is of shimmering blue velvet. I cannot imagine any royal couple looking finer than Lord and Lady Milton this evening!

After the children are asleep, I run a bath and luxuriate in taking as much hot water as I wish. There is no one to knock on the door to tell me to hurry up, or to remind me not to use up all the hot water!

When I emerge, Mrs. Landers is just bringing in a jug of cocoa and a plate of biscuits. "By this time tomorrow," she informs me, "we will have made our last stop before we leave the Irish coast and head out to open waters. Your first sight of land, Miss Gardener, will be next week, when we approach New York. Sleep well, miss."

I wish Mrs. Landers hadn't reminded me that there is nothing but ocean for an entire week! Tomorrow, I will teach the girls how to put on their life jackets, and we will practice daily, until we sight land again.

This has been a wonderful day...I have been treated like a person and not like an ignorant, untrained girl, constantly in need of reproof! I pour myself a cup of cocoa and nibble a jam-filled biscuit, remembering Mr. Briggs' advice: "If the weather is rough, Gardener, eat nothing but an apple for breakfast and a small digestive biscuit. Then, take a brisk walk on deck."

Rough? I can barely feel the throb of the engines. The ship moves as smoothly as if it were a toy boat, adrift on the lake in Hyde Park.

"Are you dreaming, Gardener?" Hart asks. I have not seen her since before lunch. She comes in, flops down in the other armchair, takes off her shoes, and flexes her feet. I jump up, pour out a cup of cocoa, and bring it to her.

"There's no need to wait on me, Gardener, I'm

sure you are as tired as I am. What a long day it's
been. I would have been back earlier, but Lady Milton
forgot to take her fan in to dinner. Our steward said
eleven courses are served in the first-class dining
room! Her ladyship sometimes feels faint, if she has
to stand or sit for too long. I ran down to D deck to
take her the fan. Luckily Lady Milton had not yet left
the white paneled reception room. I waited behind,
so I could take a quick peek at the dining room. It
is beautiful beyond words, Gardener: sparkling sil-
verware, gold-rimmed wine glasses on snow white
linen tablecloths. The crew must be busy day and
night. Every table is laid to perfection, with arrange-
ments of fresh flowers and candles. The fruit bowls
just spill over with oranges, grapes, peaches, and
plums. I wish Mr. Briggs could see that room. Even
he could not fault anything.

"Seating is at round tables for six to eight guests,
and there are romantic alcoves for two or four. And
the orchestra plays during dinner!"

I like listening to Hart talk–she does not put on
airs, even though she is Lady Milton's personal maid.
I was afraid she might resent having to share a room
with me!

"Lady Milton is pleasant to work for," Hart continues. "It's natural with the baby coming that she tires
more easily. I am so relieved to be sharing with you.
I must admit, Gardener, I was not looking forward

to rooming with Nanny Mackintosh! Don't get me wrong, I have nothing against her. I know she is very experienced and a good nanny, but–" She raises her eyebrows, and we smile at each other. Nanny is a tartar and everyone knows it! It is kind of Hart to make me feel at ease.

"I admit I was afraid of sharing with you, Hart, but not anymore," I say, losing my shyness.

"I'm glad to hear that. Did you think I've always been a lady's maid, Gardener? I started out when I was twelve years old. My first household had a cook, a maid, and no other help. I never stopped running from morning to night. They gave all the worst jobs to me. That was twelve years ago, and I've been with Lord and Lady Milton for five years. It took me a while to work myself up! But you are going to get on. I can see that Lady Milton has taken a liking to you!"

Now I feel shy again. "Hart, do you eat in the dining room, after the lords and ladies have left?"

"No, the first-class maids and valets eat in a saloon, next to the doctor's office on C deck. It's like the servants' hall, except that it's all new. We are waited on by stewards and are served the same food as the second-class passengers. That's five courses–a good variety and more than I can manage.

"I was thinking, you should have a bit of time for yourself of an evening. You might like to meet the servants or take a walk on deck. I don't mind watching the girls for an hour, once her ladyship has gone to dinner. She won't be back until late. She'll take a stroll, have coffee in the reading room, or attend a concert."

"Thank you very much, Hart. I'd love to take a walk after the girls are asleep."

"One or two of the valets are very nice-looking. You should come into the saloon," she teases.

"Are the valets as handsome as Mr. Harris is, Hart? I can tell he likes you!" I say.

This conversation reminds me of Kathleen and me, whispering in our bedroom at home so as not to wake up Emily.

"I know," she sighs. "But it won't do. It always causes friction in the household, and the other servants gossip. Mrs. Ransom and Mr. Briggs would not approve if we started walking out together. And I want to keep my place. I know when I'm well off.

"There's a lady in suite 52-3—that's the biggest suite on B deck—with its own private promenade deck! She brought fourteen trunks on board, can you imagine? And we know who had to pack them—her maid! The lady is a tyrant, not a bit like Lady Milton. And I've seen the maid tremble whenever her mistress speaks to her. Shouted at and berated from the minute she gets up, I should think. No, I intend for things to stay just the way they are."

"But what if you were to get married?" I ask, hoping she won't think I am impertinent.

"I don't know, though I admit Mr. Harris is nice. And how about Mr. Phipps, then? I've noticed him looking at you. He's a bit smitten, I think." I can feel myself blush and change the subject.

"Mrs. Landers said if we put our shoes in the corridor, the night steward will brush them. I'll take them now." I go out hastily, hoping Hart has not noticed my hot cheeks.

I wake up early next morning. For a minute, I don't know where I am. Last night I thought I'd never go to sleep, but the hum of the engines and the gentle motion of the ship soon had me drifting dreamlessly. I jump out of bed and open the door just wide enough to pick up our shoes, shined to perfection. Hart is already up. I hurry to dress before Mrs. Landers comes in. I have just finished braiding my hair when she knocks on the door and brings our early-morning tea. Hart pours it.

"I still have ten minutes before the dress bugle sounds. I shall have to watch that I don't get too used to being spoiled like this! What a lovely change, being brought our tea instead of having to carry up the morning trays," Hart says, biting into a scone.

"Gardy?" Miss Alexandra is always the first one in the morning to call me.

"Is that what they call you?" Hart says. "Nanny Mackintosh does not approve of pet names, but I think it's nice. It shows the children have taken to you." She straightens her cap and cuffs and hurries out, just as the bugle sounds.

Our breakfast of porridge, bacon, eggs, sausages, toast, butter, and jam arrives. Miss Portia asks, "Is it Sunday?" Bacon is a rare Sunday treat in our nursery.

"No, it is Thursday, but you may have sausage or bacon when you have finished your porridge. I do believe that Chef thinks every day is Sunday!" I say, enjoying the delicious food as much as the children.

"I shall ask Papa if we may live here forever," Miss Portia says.

I remove a sausage from Miss Alexandra and remind her, "Porridge first!"

After breakfast is over, I look out the window at perfect blue skies. "We musn't waste that lovely April sunshine. As soon as we have tried on our life jackets, we will go and explore the ship. We have lots more things to see," I say.

"Don't want to," Miss Alexandra says, pushing away the cork jacket I hold ready.

"It is too hot." Miss Portia turns her back to me. Not for nothing have I helped Mother with Emily and my brothers!

"What a pity," I say. "I was hoping to tell Captain Smith that you can put your life jackets on faster than anyone on board!" The thought of my speaking to this grand bearded gentleman, in his gold braided uniform surrounded by officers and admiring passengers, makes me quake. Luckily the girls do not know that!

Before I have time to count to three, they are scrambling to push their arms through the jackets. Miss Portia manages to tie hers up while I fasten Miss Alexandra's.

"Close your eyes and open your mouths," I whisper, and pop two of the sugar cubes I've saved for this occasion into their mouths. Sometimes bribery is justified. If Nanny Mackintosh was ever to find out about my method of child-rearing, I have no doubt I'd be dismissed on the spot!

"You may take off the jackets now. We shall play this game every day, and each time, you will have a sugar lump. Now we are going to explore. Mrs. Landers told me about an alleyway the crew use to get from one end of the ship to the other. None of the passengers knows about it. The crew are as quiet and invisible as little mice, I'm told."

In the lift, I ask for E deck.

"If you are wanting the swimming bath and Turkish baths, miss, you will find them on F deck!" the lift boy says, about to press the wrong button.

"No, E deck, if you please," I repeat.

The boy blushes. *Oh, dear, I did not mean to sound cross.*

"I beg your pardon, miss," he says. *He must think I am a difficult passenger!*

"I have to deliver a letter, you see, to a member of the crew," I explain.

"Certainly, miss, my mistake," he says, not looking at me, and presses the correct button.

The alley is a long plain corridor, with walls tiled in white from deck to ceiling. Every few yards are iron staircases. I have no idea where they lead to. *How am I going to find Patrick?* I don't know if I will even recognize him. I have only met him once!

Suddenly the girls let go of my hands, rush forward, and kneel down beside a cat.

"Cat, good kitty," they croon. I crouch down beside them, and we stroke the plump gray creature that has appeared so mysteriously.

"Wherever did you come from?" I say.

A voice above me says, "I might ask you the same thing, young ladies. Have you lost your way?"

I jump up, straightening my skirts. A young man wearing a long striped apron over his uniform looks down at us. Flustered, I try to explain. "I am looking for someone, a Mr. Patrick O'Connor. I have promised to deliver a letter to him from my sister."

Two stewards glance at us curiously as they pass by, their arms full of neatly folded linen. A sailor clambers up one of the iron staircases–it is busier down here than on the Grand Staircase!

"Never heard of him, miss, but that's not surprising. We are a crew of 685. Which department does he work in?"

"He is a stoker," I reply.

"No one is allowed down there, miss. It's hot and dangerous, with the furnaces blazing and sparks flying. Tell you what, give me your letter and I'll do my best to make sure he gets it.

"Now then, our Jenny..." He picks up the cat and talks tenderly to her. "You should be getting back to your quarters. The boys will be looking for you, worrying about you. Miss Jenny will have kittens any day now. That's considered a lucky omen on a maiden voyage," he says.

"And now, ladies, you must excuse me. This alley is only for the crew. I'll walk you back to the lift."

A white-coated waiter with a laden tray hurries past us. "Chef told me to send you straight back. He's running short of glasses," he says.

"I am sorry," I say. "I did not mean to get you into trouble, but I promised my sister." *Why can't I ever learn my place?* Miss Portia fondles Jenny's ears, and the cat purrs loudly.

"Is Jenny your cat?" Miss Portia asks.

"In a manner of speaking, Jenny belongs to all of us—she is the ship's cat. You need a cat on board to keep the mice and rats away.

"And now, ladies, you'll need to return to your deck. The ship will be docking in Queenstown soon to take on the last of our passengers. A hundred expected—mainly immigrants for steerage, I hear, bound for America. By late afternoon, it will be full speed ahead for the Statue of Liberty and New York. That is a fine sight, I can tell you. With a bit of luck and the fair weather holding, we are hoping to get in a day early. There is nothing like being out on the open sea, never knowing from one day to the next what the weather will bring."

This is the second time I am reminded that we will soon be out of sight of land! My expression must give me away.

The young man says, "Think of the ship as a small town, miss. The decks are your streets, paved with wood instead of cobblestones. They're as safe and watertight as your own house." He obviously does not know what our scullery is like at home, and how it floods when we have a rainstorm!

"Here we are. The lift will be along any minute."

"Thank you very much, Mr...?"

"I'm Tim, one of the glass-washers. I won't forget your letter. Chef will be sending out a search party for me!" He hurries away.

The girls talk about Jenny for the rest of the morning.

———

At Queenstown, we stop to watch the long line of passengers going up the third-class gangway. There are many children among them—we have very few in first class. It seems a pity that gates separate us all. Father would say everyone is happiest keeping to their own place, but I do not believe that is true. On the first day, when passengers from second class were allowed to explore the ship, I noticed a nice-looking girl with her little brother and sister. I would have liked to have someone my own age to talk to.

The seagulls are noisy and fight over bits of leftover food from our lunches, which have been thrown overboard.

Later in the afternoon, I take the children up to A deck to see their mother in the Verandah Café and Palm Court. The air is still full of birds beating their wings steadily, following behind the ship as she steams, proudly, through the calm Atlantic waters.

I wander to the end of the promenade deck and look down on B deck below. On the stern of the ship—the back or aft, as it's called—a man plays the bagpipes. The music is as mournful as if he were playing at a funeral. *Is he a passenger who came aboard at Queenstown?* He plays as if his heart were broken, bidding farewell as the coast of Ireland gradually disappears and the sun begins to fade.

It makes me sad to listen and I shiver, even in my warm coat. The wailing of the bagpipes somehow reminds me of Lady Portman's garden, of the voices that called to me in the night air, crying from the depths of the water.

I am glad to return to the café–it is time to fetch the children. I pay only surface attention to the girls' chatter.

Miss Portia scolds me. "You are not listening, Gardy. We had ice cream and strawberries!"

"You never did! You must be dreaming–strawberries in April, in the middle of the ocean?"

"Yes, yes!" Miss Alexandra nods her head vigorously.

"Indeed, it is true, Gardy," her sister says.

"Indeed, is it? Then you must be the luckiest children in the whole world. Did you save some for me?"

"All gone." Miss Alexandra looks wistful, but I doubt it is on my account.

Just as we turn to go down the staircase, we pass the nanny who avoided us earlier. The little girl with her waves to Miss Alexandra, but the nanny hurries her away, saying, "Come along, do, Miss Loraine."

The week passes pleasantly, the weather remains beautiful, the sun shines every day, and true to Mrs. Landers' prediction, the *Titanic* is a happy ship!

On Saturday evening, Hart looks particularly smart as she goes in to have her dinner in the saloon.

"You do look nice, Hart," I tell her.

"There's to be a bit of a party tonight, seeing tomorrow is Sunday, so I have to look my best. I'll be back in plenty of time for you to have your moonlight stroll, Gardener."

Kathleen was right about there always being a moon! I like my walks on deck, and it is surprising how many of the passengers I have come to know by sight, or to say "good evening" to. There is an elderly couple who always walk arm in arm—they are inseparable. Hart told me they are a Mr. and Mrs. Straus, who own Macy's, a big department store in New York. Mrs. Straus always greets me. She reminds me of the woman at the shoe stall where Mother buys our boots.

Little Robert Spedden's nanny sometimes walks with me, and we laugh at the young couple on their honeymoon because they argue so often! It was she who told me about the second Mrs. Astor, who never smiles in public. I don't wonder. Mrs. Astor must know her in-laws don't think she is good enough for Colonel Astor. He is supposedly the richest man on board ship! Everyone on the *Titanic*, at least in first class, knows everyone else and their secrets. Obviously they have never heard of Nanny Mackintosh's warning, never to discuss one's private life.

I did mention my suspicions to Hart about the nanny I think is Roberts.

"There is nothing we can do, Gardener. We have no proof that she stole anything, and she might say that you are being spiteful, or worse. I say, give her a chance to start a new life. If she is unkind to those little children, it will be discovered soon enough, and she will be dismissed!"

Tonight I walk along our deck, past the Café Parisien, where the waiters converse in French. The ship's orchestra trio plays tunes that get my feet tapping! I wish Kathleen were here with me to watch the elegant passengers, laughing, talking, and drinking wine. I'll always remember how the air is filled with the scent of perfume and the smell of the gentlemen's cigars.

Tomorrow is our fifth day on board. Sunday service will be led by Captain Smith in the first-class saloon, after breakfast. And in only three more days—less, if Mr. Ismay, the managing director of the White Star Line, gets his way—we reach New York!

The *Titanic* will have set a new record for the crossing. As for me, though this whole voyage seems like a dream, I shall be more than happy to arrive back home in England!

13

Sunday, April 14

Our first Sunday at sea feels special. I dress the girls in their new cream-colored frocks. The children look a picture, sitting between their parents, waiting patiently for Captain Smith to begin the service. I can't help smiling, thinking of Miss Portia asking me if she should wear her life jacket to show the captain how quickly she can put it on!

Hart and I sit at the back of the first-class saloon, with the other servants. I look around for Roberts— almost certain that it is her—but she is not here. However, Miss Loraine sits between her mother and father, just behind Miss Alexandra, who turns around to smile and wave at the little girl.

One should think kindly of everyone on a Sunday, but I can't help wondering if Roberts found an excuse to stay with the baby boy. She must know, by now, that her former employers are on board and that even a wig, dyed hair, or a nurse's uniform cannot disguise her forever!

When we stand to sing

> *Eternal Father, strong to save...*
> *O hear us when we cry to Thee*
> *For those in peril on the sea,*

the words have never sounded more beautiful to me, especially because we have the ship's orchestra to accompany us. The service does not end until noon, but the children have behaved beautifully throughout. Captain Smith shakes hands with all the passengers, and I am as thrilled as Miss Portia and Miss Alexandra are to be included.

It must have been the hymn that gives me the idea to take the children up to the boat deck to look at the lifeboats.

"Look, here they all are. Can you read what name is written on each side, Miss Portia? I will give you a clue. The lifeboats have the same name as our ship," I say.

"I know, I know, it is *Titanic!* I can read, Gardy," she says proudly.

"Me read too, *Titanic,*" Miss Alexandra repeats, not to be outdone.

"You are both very clever girls. Now, look at the numbers 2, 4, 6, 8, 10, 12, 14, and 16–these are the even numbers. They are on our left, which the crew calls the port side, Mrs. Landers said. And on our right, on the starboard side, are the odd numbers: 1, 3, 5, 7, 9, 11, 13, and 15." This is far too much information for the children to take in, but I do it as much for myself as for them. It is a precaution. There is no harm in looking at the *Titanic*'s safety features!

The boat deck is deserted. Other passengers are wiser than me, for the wind has turned bitter and the temperature has dropped.

"Let's run along one side of the deck and then down the other, before lunch. It will warm us up." I hold out my hands. A gust of wind blows off my cap, and my hair tumbles down. The children shriek with merriment, and we almost collide with Mr. Thomas Andrews. I had not noticed his lonely figure before.

"I do beg your pardon, sir," I say.

"This belongs to you, I believe, Nanny?" Mr. Andrews says, and returns my cap. "And do you still like my ship, young ladies?" he asks the children.

They nod vigorously, suddenly shy.

"You need not be concerned, Nanny. There are twenty lifeboats, including the four Englehardt collapsibles. Not that we have need of so many. As it is, we have room for quite half the passengers–more than the law asks of us. In addition, I designed sixteen

watertight compartments. They reach all the way up
to F deck. You may rest assured, the *Titanic* is unsinkable! I wish you a pleasant afternoon." He bows and
continues on his walk.

Mr. Andrews is such a kind gentleman. *To think
that he would stop and talk to me!* Now, Mr. Ismay of
the White Star Line walks past us as though we are
invisible. I have not been given so much as a nod,
though we often pass by him in the corridor. His
stateroom is also on B deck.

Hart said that Mr. Ismay's manservant mentioned
that his employer's sole topic of conversation is taken
up with beating the competition. He keeps urging
the captain to increase the ship's speed! As if it mat-
tered whether we get to New York a few hours earlier
or later...

"I'm cold," Miss Alexandra says, shivering.

"I am too. Come along into the lift and down to
our warm stateroom. Won't it be lovely to eat some
nice hot soup for lunch?" I say.

The sun has disappeared and it feels almost cold
enough to snow. When Hart comes in after lunch,
she says that I should not bring the girls up to the
Verandah Café and Palm Court this afternoon. Lady
Milton has decided it is too chilly.

"I have not seen anyone out on deck," Hart says,
"but the library and little writing room are full. There
is to be a big dinner party this evening, in the à la

carte restaurant, which the first-class passengers have named the Ritz. The dinner is to be in honor of Captain Smith's last voyage before he retires. Lord and Lady Milton have been invited. Lord Milton has already been down to the purser's office to fetch Lady Milton's diamond tiara, bracelet, and necklace. There will be more glittering jewelry at that dinner party, Gardener, than you'd find at Buckingham Palace or Windsor Castle! And as for the food, goodness knows what has been ordered specially for the occasion. I shall ask her ladyship to tell me. Mrs. Porter is sure to be interested."

"Don't you think it is wasteful, Hart, to spend all that money up there when they serve such wonderful food in the first-class dining saloon?"

"What do we understand of the whims of American millionaires? I am more than satisfied with the meals we are served in the saloon—fit for the grandest home, I should think!" Hart says.

"Mrs. Landers says Chef sends up plain, simple, nursery meals for us. He has no idea what is meant by plain nursery food, and I'm happy to admit it. Last night, we had chocolate éclairs for dessert. I had never tasted them before! You should have seen Miss Alexandra's face—chocolate from eyebrows to chin! Can you imagine what Nanny Mackintosh would have said?"

"Don't get too used to all of this, Gardener," Hart

says. "We'll be returning to normal soon and to eating good plain English food. I'm not complaining—we are luckier than some I know, where the cook watches every scrap of butter the servants put on their toast! We are treated fairly. I'm not just talking about food. What I'm trying to say is, nothing about the way life runs in our household at Number 4, or anywhere else, is going to change, Gardener. We'll go on the same way we've always done."

"I know that, Hart. No one could live like this; it's not real life!" I am glad Hart reminded me that all I am is a fourteen-year-old nursemaid who'll soon be back at the house as an extra pair of hands for Nanny Mackintosh. But that's what I was hired to be. No one ever promised me anything different.

You're right, Father. It's about keeping to my place. I can't help hearing his voice in my head—I do need to be reminded. *To think I had not wanted to come!* Well, I have had my wish—I have seen what the world is like and how different it can be. But the whole ship is not like first class. I know about the stokers, who live and work in the bowels of the ship. The sailors and cooks and glass-washers and stewards, they are the ones—the servants, like Hart and me—who make first class happen.

As Mother said, "There are those at the top and those at the bottom of the heap."

"Thanks, Hart, maybe I have been carried away a bit. But I've enjoyed myself as much as the children!"

"You've been a tonic for those little girls. Anyone can see how fond you are of them. Look at the time! I must go. I've to press Lady Milton's dinner gown, her newest one, bought especially for the voyage. A lovely, dusty-rose-colored silk, with an embroidered bodice and matching shoes. I will see you tonight, though if it gets any colder, you would be better off in the servants' saloon than walking on deck and freezing to death!"

It is kind of Hart to give me this time to myself every evening. She does not need to do that, and I would never have asked her. She was right about the cold. Tonight I stay out hardly any time at all and am soon driven back to our stateroom. Hart crouches by the electric heater, and I sit beside her, warming my frozen fingers.

"You want to be careful not to be blown overboard on a night like this, Gardener. I'll go down to the saloon for a bit, just to show my face. I'll be back up long before her ladyship returns, after the concert."

The girls lie curled up beside each other, just like Kathleen and I used to do. I cover them with an extra blanket, then lay out their warmest clothes for the morning, adding flannel petticoats. The life jackets are on the chairs, arranged as I have done since our first night on board. The little sisters compete now for who can put on their jacket first and who will receive the first sugar cube.

I told them earlier, "I declare you have eaten so much Sunday dinner, I shall have to ask for adult-size life jackets for you both!" They giggled, puffed out their cheeks, and strutted round the cabin, enjoying the joke.

Our Sunday night dinner of roast lamb and mint sauce, as well as chicken or beef, salads, vegetables, and new potatoes, would last our family for a week. You would think that Chef grows a garden on deck! As well as ice cream and oranges in jelly, Mrs. Landers brought in a fruit basket crammed with every imaginable fruit, even purple grapes the size of plums! "Every table in the dining rooms, for all three classes, has a similar basket," she said, "as a centerpiece for Sunday night."

I'm afraid Mrs. Wilson will not only have to lengthen the hems of my uniforms, but also let out the seams....

I close the door of the children's room. The girls have not stirred. I feel restless—it has been quiet tonight, passengers retiring early because of the change in the weather. Our hot chocolate is waiting on the table, and Mrs. Landers has brought in a dish of biscuits as usual, but I am too full to nibble even one. I put my feet up on a chair and lean back on the sofa, waiting for Hart to return. She often has some interesting gossip to tell me!

I must have dozed off to the steady throb of the ship's engines. But suddenly I wake up as if someone had nudged me, the kind of jolt that occurs when Mr. Harris stops the automobile unexpectedly. A scraping sound fills my ears–sharp as nails across a blackboard, yet distant, as if a grand piano were being dragged carelessly across a polished floor. *Why would someone be moving furniture at this time? And how can I manage to hear it when there is carpet everywhere?* Something else must be causing the noise.

I look out into the corridor, and a few other passengers do the same. A gentleman wearing his dressing gown peers round his cabin door, before closing it again. There is nothing unusual at all, except that just as I am getting ready to go to bed, I notice that the engines have stopped. I stand still, listening to the unaccustomed silence replacing the hum of working engines. I go to the window and look out.

The night sky is brilliant with stars, then a dark shadow looms up close and drifts past. I remember Lord Milton's words when we stopped moving that first day out of Southampton. He said that it was a close shave after the *Titanic* had started to move again. But now we are well on our way to New York, with the whole ocean to sail on. *What could possibly get in the way of our ship?* A gong booms from one end of the ship to the other—*is it a warning of some kind?* Moments later, Hart bustles in.

"Not in bed yet, Gardener? It is nice and warm in here. You'll never guess what I brought to show you, look!" She holds out her hand, with a piece of ice beginning to melt in her palm. "There are more pieces on deck." Hart warms her hands in front of the heater. *Something strange is happening. Nothing feels right....*

"Did you hear that gong sounding a minute ago?" I ask her. Hart shrugs her shoulders.

"There was quite a party going on in the third-class saloon. Some of the lads sounded the gong for a lark—I shouldn't be a bit surprised!" she says. "We could hear them singing and dancing earlier, before the steward switched off their lights at eleven o'clock! It will soon be midnight, and I'm off to my bed. Lady Milton is fast asleep, and Lord Milton has gone up to smoke a last cigar." She yawns.

Footsteps hurry up and down the corridor, followed by a knock on the door. Mrs. Landers does not wait for a reply, but enters and says, "No need for alarm, ladies."

I feel certain she means the exact opposite!

"Captain Smith has requested all passengers to go up on the boat deck and to bring their life jackets. It is only a precaution, he said. There is nothing to worry about." Our stewardess disappears before we have a chance to ask her any questions. The engines have not started up again.

"I will see you and the girls on deck, Gardener. I must wake Lady Milton and help her dress–she will need her furs. I hope Lord Milton has returned from the smoking room," Hart says.

"Hart, wait, put your coat on! And take your life jacket," I say, reaching up to get it down for her from the top of the wardrobe.

"I'll come back for it later. No doubt it is only a drill, our first one! Though why they would choose a cold Sunday night..."

After Hart leaves, a kind of calm settles over me. I have a premonition that something beyond my control is about to happen. *Is this the moment I have been preparing for, without knowing it?* Deep down, my mistrust of the sea is always there, waiting to surface.

I wake up the sleepy children and dress them. They raise and lower their arms obediently, helping me to put on their life jackets over their coats.

"Look at us, dressing in the middle of the night because Captain Smith wants us to go on deck so he can count the passengers!" I say. "Come along now, and very soon your mama and papa and Hart will join us." I put on my own coat and life jacket and, before leaving the cabin, wrap a few biscuits in a napkin and thrust them deep into the pockets of my coat. We may be on deck for some time!

"Is this a game?" Miss Portia asks.

"A kind of game," I reply.

When we go out in the corridor, ladies and gentlemen are laughing and joking as if it is the most natural thing in the world to go up on deck at a time when normally we'd all be asleep.

One lady who is draped in a blanket asks her steward if she is expected to go up too. "I have a cold," she says, "I would like some tea with lemon, if you please."

"Don't you worry, madam, you will all be back on board by morning," he replies, continuing down the corridor.

"Then I intend to wait and see what morning brings—after I am suitably dressed and have eaten my breakfast," she says to his retreating form and goes back into her room, shutting the door behind her.

It sounds as if we may be going on the lifeboats! I hurry the children toward the lift. All around us, passengers are emerging in the strangest assortment of clothes. Furs over night attire, one lady in her slippers, another carrying several shawls and a hatbox! Stewards are still knocking on cabin doors, smiling, and speaking reassuringly: "No cause for alarm, madam, sir!" I'm beginning to wonder if they really know what is going on.

A portly gentleman, still dressed in his evening clothes, takes hold of a steward's arm. "Look here, my good man, why has the captain not made an announcement to the passengers? Not very sporting, keeping us in the dark like this!" The lift arrives and the door opens. He enters in front of us, making sure he and his wife have enough room. I follow them in.

We are packed together tightly, and I pick up Miss Alexandra. Another gentleman comforts his wife, "This is a mere formality, my dear, you must not upset yourself! If anything was really amiss, we would have been notified."

Outside, on deck, the cold takes my breath away. I turn up the collars of our coats.

"Where is the moon gone, Gardy?"

"It is late, after midnight; I expect the moon is asleep!"

We hold on to each other's hands tightly. Miss Alexandra is already shivering with cold. I scan the deck, hoping to see Lord and Lady Milton and Hart.

The lift brings up more and more passengers. A group waits near us, trying to get some information from the officers. They are too busy to answer, directing and instructing the crew, who have begun to lower the lifeboats on the starboard side. I think I recognize the girl I saw on the first day, standing with her young brother and sister, though it is difficult to make out faces clearly. *What are the second-class passengers doing up here, if there is nothing amiss?*

The most wonderful aroma of freshly baked bread is in the air. Two of the pantry boys have brought up baskets of bread. Anyone would think we are about to have a midnight picnic! Miss Portia tugs at my hand. She wants to look over the railing and stands on tiptoe to do so. I grip her by the back of her life jacket with one hand. With the other, I clutch Miss Alexandra, who is doing her best to follow her sister.

A lifeboat hovers in midair, being let down inch by inch, ropes creaking in the wind. The blackness of the water so far below us makes me dizzy. I hear an officer asking the ladies to enter the boat. He calls out in vain. *Who wants to leave our beautiful ship to step down into that nothingness?* A hissing noise erupts as steam shoots out of the funnels, adding to the clamor on deck. If only there was someone to tell us what to do...

14

Women and Children First

"Women and children first, please," says the officer in charge. He sounds like a salesman pushing his wares, trying to coax unwilling customers to purchase his goods.

But no one wants to leave the *Titanic*. *Why would they?* A gentleman nearby urges his wife to go. I overhear his wife say, "Nonsense, Herbert, I refuse to enter one of those small wooden boats, not on someone's whim. No, don't tell me again that you think we have struck an iceberg—it makes no difference. We will be safer on board!" They move off.

An iceberg! Could it be true? Hart did show me a piece of ice, but Mrs. Landers would have told us if there was any danger. And I believe in Mr. Andrews. He said the ship is watertight. However, it is too cold for the children to stay out here any longer!

"Come along, my dears, we will go to the gymnasium. It will be nice and warm in there and much easier for your mama and papa to find us." *What can be taking them so long?*

Several passengers, encouraged by the gymnasium instructor, are using the stationary bicycles and rowing machines. Music wafts in from the deck. The orchestra must have come up to play. I recognize the melody–Mr. Phipps has been known to whistle it. He said it is the latest American composition, called "Alexander's Ragtime Band."

Miss Alexandra immediately stamps her feet and claps her hands in time to the music. A lady smiles at her indulgently. I rub my hands–icy inside my gloves–and for a few seconds, take my eyes off the child. *I should know better!* I see her dart outside again, in search of the music.

"Miss Portia, I want you to be a good, brave girl and stay right here. I will be back as fast as I can. I must find your sister," I say.

"Please don't leave me, Gardy," she says with a sob. I am tempted not to, but taking her with me would cause delay. The instructor and several passengers are close by.

"I must, Miss Portia. I will be back as soon as I can, I promise!" I swallow my panic. *I will find her, of course I will.* I run out, looking from one side of the deck to the other. How dark and gloomy it looks compared to the brightness of the gymnasium. Many more passengers have arrived on deck. The blackness of the sky, despite the brilliance of the stars, is bewildering after the light and warmth of the gymnasium. I feel as if I am chasing shadows....

A dog barks, poking his small head out of a lady's muff. Most of the animals on board live below the passenger decks, in kennels and cages. Stewards and crew members walk the dogs during the day. I like to look down on them as they walk round and round on the second-class promenade. I must concentrate. *Where would she go?*

"Oh, where are you, Alexandra?" *Who are all these people?* I think I see her and call out her name, but the small figure in its dark blue coat and bonnet disappears into the gloom. I make my way towards the orchestra. Surely, that is where she will be.

I make a silent promise that I will never, ever allow such a thing to happen again. Nanny Mackintosh was right not to trust me!

Suddenly, rockets flare up into the sky, blazing like fireworks on Guy Fawkes Night! For a moment, the crowd moves with and against each other, not knowing what to do or where to go. We all realize this is a call for help. The *Titanic* is sending a signal to the world of her distress!

The danger is real–I must find Miss Alexandra. *Suppose Miss Portia gets tired of waiting and comes to look for us? The three of us separated!*

Crewmen tug at ropes and run back and forth, shouting instructions to each other. More passengers crowd onto the deck, jostling for space. They are laden with boxes and parcels, speaking in a babble of languages. The children, none of whom I have seen before, are bewildered and cling to their mothers' skirts. In despair, I call out Miss Alexandra's name over and over again.

What if she falls? What if she is trampled in the confusion of bodies and luggage? She is so little, no one will notice her! A woman, at the far end of the deck, begins to play the harmonica. Her children gather around her, and in the next flare of rockets, I catch a glimpse of golden curls. A small hand waves her bonnet in the air. Hoping she will hear me this time, I scream her name again.

The deck slopes to one side. I trip over bundles, right myself, and reach Miss Alexandra at last. I pick her up and hold her tight, not knowing whether to kiss or shake her! I am so relieved to have her safe again in my arms.

"No, no," she howls, wanting to stay.

"That is quite enough. Come along, Miss Alexandra, we are going back to your sister! How can you be so naughty and run away?" I put her down and grasp her hand firmly. My voice sounds exactly like Nanny Mackintosh's.

Miss Alexandra looks at me angelically. "More dance?" she asks, hopefully.

"Not now, Miss Alexandra." I tie on her bonnet again, and we make our way back to the gymnasium. The light beckons to us. *If only Portia has waited! How long have we been away?* The gymnasium is almost empty now, and there is no sign of Lord and Lady Milton or of Hart. Miss Portia is huddled on the floor, her back against the wall. We crouch down beside her. I pull her hands down gently from her face and wipe her cheeks, which are damp with tears. I have seen Emmy do the same, believing it makes her invisible. I am overcome with guilt and fear. *Will we all see our families again?* Miss Alexandra pats her sister's arm.

"There now, Miss Portia, you didn't think I had broken my promise, did you? I would never leave you, never, and your sister is very sorry, are you not?"

"Yes," Miss Alexandra says and puts her thumb in her mouth.

Groping for a handkerchief in my pocket, I find the package of biscuits. "Shall we have a little treat?" I give them each a biscuit and wrap the remaining ones up again. We may not be back in our cabin for breakfast after all!

"Now, put your mittens on. We will see if Mama and Papa are waiting outside."

As we emerge on the port side, a crowd of passengers waits to climb into the remaining lifeboats. More than half the boats have already left. I hope that Lord and Lady Milton are safe on one of them!

By the light of the next flare, I see the boats rowing slowly away from the ship, bobbing in the sea like wooden toys.

"Women and children first!" the officer in charge of loading the next lifeboat shouts. We join a line of passengers. I have no choice except to get the girls safely away. Hart will have told their parents that we had left the cabin to go on deck. I don't know how we could have missed each other. Looking around for them again, I see so many passengers waiting–hundreds of people! *Will there be room for all of us?*

What was it Mr. Andrews said? That there is room in the lifeboats for half our passengers? Then what is to happen to those who cannot find a place? The boats must intend to return for more passengers. In response to the flares, ships will arrive to rescue us. *But what are we being rescued from? No one has told us what is happening!* The *Titanic*'s deck slopes more now, but there is no one to ask what it means.

A shot rings out. The woman standing in front of me, her arm linked to that of an old lady, makes the sign of the cross with her free hand. "May God have mercy on our souls," she says.

Her companion refuses to move, holding up the line. A sailor lifts the old woman in his arms and drops her, protesting, the few feet from the deck into the boat.

"I'm coming, Ma," her daughter calls, hoisting up her skirts.

I pick up Miss Alexandra. "Whatever happens, Miss Portia," I say, "keep hold of my coat and don't let go."

"In you get, lassies, boat 12," a sailor says, wrenching Miss Alexandra from my arms. He lowers her to a woman already seated below and shouts to the officer in charge, "Thirty-eight passengers aboard, sir."

"We'll take six more, then. Move the rest of the line over to boat 14. I'm giving the order to board, now!"

"Sir, please, the children's parents...Lord and Lady Milton...and their maid...did you see them?"

He shrugs. I don't think he has even heard me!

"Keep moving! Women and children only, men stand back," the officer shouts.

"I have forgotten my gold watch. I must return to my cabin," the lady behind me insists.

"Your watch will still be there tomorrow, madam. Down you go, or miss your place." She turns and leaves.

I hear Miss Alexandra shrieking my name above the uproar.

It is our turn now. The line has dwindled and formed anew in front of the remaining boats. Miss Portia pulls away from me. "Papa, Papa," she calls out.

I turn, grasping her wrist. We must stay together. Somehow Lord Milton has pushed his way through to us! Oh, I am so relieved to see him.

"Look after them, Gardener, I promised my wife...." He grasps Miss Portia's hand, then releases it. *Isn't he coming with us?* His words become lost in a confusion of shouts and orders. He disappears among the crowd of men and crew before I have a chance to beg him to stay with us.

"Keep the men back and move along. Lower number 14," the officer barks.

Miss Portia and I clamber into boat number 12, clinging to each other. Once down, I pick up Miss Alexandra from the woman's knee. We manage to squeeze into a cramped space and sit together. Miss Portia and I search the darkness above us, hoping for another glimpse of Lord Milton.

Miss Portia clutches a card. "Papa gave it to me. 'This is for Roger,' he said." I wait for another flare's light to read by. It is Lord Milton's boarding pass, and I can just make out the words:

WHITE STAR LINE

BOARDING PASS

PERMISSION GRANTED TO COME ABOARD

WHITE STAR LINE'S

R. M. S. TITANIC

A girl stumbles over my legs; we both mumble an apology. I button the card inside Miss Portia's pocket. The boat begins to descend with a rocking motion—the journey has begun, down from the top-most deck and into the ocean below. *Was it only five or six days ago that we embarked?* The first time I looked up at the ship from the dock at Southampton, I marveled at its height. And now, from this height, we must descend. My mouth is dry with fear.

The women whisper to their little ones. Someone moans. Miss Alexandra chuckles, "Lift go down, lift down!" I hold Miss Portia's hand tightly and bury my face in the back of Miss Alexandra's neck.

Inch by inch, we are lowered into the sea. The orchestra plays on, accompanying the creaking of the ropes. The lifeboat swings dizzily from side to side, jerks, stops, descends once more. And sud-denly it is over, like a miracle! I raise my head and look around. We float on the surface of the water as dark as night, barely causing a ripple in the sea. *We have not drowned!*

The sailors take up the oars, and we slowly pull away from the ship. A flare shows us other boats some distance away, waiting, drifting. The next life-boat is lowered. Gradually, the silence in ours is broken. My neighbor counts the beads of her rosary over and over again, whispering her prayers.

Another woman sobs her despair. "They would not

open the gates for us below until the very last moment. What of our men and the others left behind?" She holds her baby, wrapped in a shawl, and weeps.

A voice answers her: "Hush now, what kind of talk is that? The officer said that once we are safely on board the ships coming to our aid, the lifeboats have orders to row back. They will rescue the others. Do you think the captain would let them drown?"

All this time, the sounds of the orchestra have carried over the water. But now I hear another melody—*is it the woman who played the harmonica? Why is she still on board the* Titanic, *instead of on a lifeboat? I thought they said women and children first?*

"Will Papa and Mama be on the next boat?" Miss Portia asks, wriggling closer to me and holding my arm as if I might vanish. *How do I answer her?* Miss Alexandra begins to fidget. I know that if I let go of her, she could easily fall overboard!

"Do you remember all the lifeboats I showed you this afternoon, Miss Portia?" *Was it this afternoon, or yesterday? I can't remember.* My feet are numb inside my shoes. I try to shield Miss Alexandra from the cold with the hem of my coat and rub her fingers inside her mittens. "I hope your mama and papa and Hart are on one of the other lifeboats, safe like us!"

A small girl without a bonnet tries to protect her ears, mottled red and purple from the wind. Her mother shelters her, as best she can, with a bit of the shawl in which she has wrapped her baby. I pull the white linen napkin from my pocket, unwrap it, and hand a biscuit to each of my girls before offering both the napkin and the last biscuit to the mother.

"*Grazie*," she says, reminding me of Mrs. Bernardi, and ties the napkin around her daughter's ears.

A lady clad in furs passes a spare shawl to a woman who is trembling with cold. She wears only a thin wrap over her nightclothes. No gates separate us, as they did on board. We are all the same now—crowded together, cold and frightened, hoping to be back on our lovely ship very soon, reunited with our friends and families.

Looking towards the *Titanic*, watching her lights shimmer across the water, I think of the steward's reassurance that we will be back on board before breakfast! I cling to the words Mr. Andrews spoke—that the *Titanic* is unsinkable. Whatever has gone wrong, he will make sure it will soon be repaired. I imagine him making notes in his little book, planning to put things right.

The lights of the *Titanic* still shine, but some of the portholes in the lower decks are dark. We have enough light to see that we are only women and children in our boat, apart from our two sailors who sit crouched over their oars. None of the other lifeboats is too far away from us. We wait, hoping for the sight of a rescue ship to take us aboard, or better still, to row us back to the *Titanic*.

15

Lost

The orchestra has been silent since the last plaintive melody wafted across the water a short while ago. The *Titanic's* lights, the beacon that gave us hope as we wait for rescue, begin to flicker on and off.

We are near enough to the ship to notice that she is leaning farther and farther towards the water. Many of the portholes are gradually disappearing. I think of some great sea monster tugging at her, refusing to let go. As the ship settles deeper and deeper, relinquishing her painful struggle, we watch, aghast, as the *Titanic's* bow sinks lower rapidly. The old woman sitting near me resumes her prayers. The clicking of her beads accompany our murmurs of disbelief.

Suddenly the air is rent with sounds such as one could never have imagined. First, one of the ship's proud funnels crashes down. And then, a thundering collision of noises rolls and slides into an avalanche of glass, mirrors, and china, breaking into a million shards!

"Don't be afraid, my dears, it is only a passing storm. Close your eyes," I tell the children. No one is prepared for such an end to the *Titanic*. It is her end, for even in the gloom of night, we sense the ship being torn in half. Sparks like shooting stars rise into the sky.

Furniture flies through the air; the sea is littered with deck chairs, doors, tables, boxes, and trunks. *Are they thrown over in hope that they may serve as life rafts?* I remember my first sight of the Grand Staircase. Now it, too, must be engulfed by waves. Nothing could remain intact in such turmoil! All of the gold and silver, the brass and ornamental carvings, tarnished by saltwater. The pride of the shipyards, of the men who built her, and of so many of us who sailed on her maiden voyage, lost....

Horror upon horror! We watch figures silhouetted against the starlit, moonless sky jump off what remains of the deck. Some men walk straight into the sea. And although our crewmen have rowed us farther away from the sinking vessel, we are still close enough to see hands gripping rails that do not hold. Men, women, and children are tossed into the ocean like rag dolls. *Is Kathleen's Patrick one of them?*

The *Titanic* is wrenched apart, and as the bow is submerged, the stern rises up, straight into the air. It soars to the sky like an arrow, poised the moment before it is released in flight, then falls. The vessel plunges into the depths of the ocean and disappears. The ship is no more....

We sit in silent darkness. A slight ripple in the water shows where the great liner vanished–all the grace, beauty, and elegance that was the *Titanic* is gone forever.

It is over, and I am ashamed to feel relieved. Sitting here, unable to help those poor people aboard, has been unbearable. No one speaks. A baby whimpers and is hushed. A splash of oars, a sob stifled. Our little boats drift to and fro, lit only by the stars. The moon has not appeared this night. There was no moon before, or after, Johnny died.

The memory is still fresh of the first time I saw the moon again, after his funeral. How it shone on the floor of our room, clear and liquid as water...*I will not think of it!* The loneliness of sitting here in our small boat, no longer able to see the *Titanic*, is like a bad dream. *How I long to wake up!*

And now the silence is broken by new sounds. From out of the darkness, pleading voices–a chorus of anguish and despair–call out, then diminish, cry by cry, frozen forever. Wreckage floats by us, bumps into the side of the boat, only to drift again, some gripped by hands that slip away before we can reach them.

The officer from lifeboat 14, the closest one to ours, takes command. He shouts to the oarsmen, "Tie the boats that are close enough together. We must make room and row back for survivors."

We try to help, cramming even closer, finding spaces. Some passengers are moved from our crowded boat, but it takes a long time in the dark for them to cross into another boat that is never quite still. I am grateful that the children and I may stay where we are. A small girl, separated from her mother in the darkness, cries bitterly.

At last, boat 14 pulls away, skirting the debris to pick up any survivors. *How long can they last in these freezing waters? How long is it since the* Titanic *sank?* All I can do to help is pray.

Lines echo in my head from the hymn we sang on Sunday morning.

> *Eternal Father, strong to save...*
> *O hear us when we cry to Thee*
> *For those in peril on the sea.*

Is He strong enough to save? Has He heard the cries? I can't remember what words come next, so I repeat the same phrases over and over again to myself.

Miss Portia whispers, "Has the singing stopped?"

I wipe the tears off my cheeks before they freeze there. "Yes," I manage to answer. My thoughts are of my little brother and the pale faces of the drowned.

Thankfully, Miss Alexandra is asleep. Her arms are fastened round my neck, her legs around my waist.

Miss Portia tugs at my sleeve. "Look, Gardy, the moon is awake again." A crescent moon appears over the horizon. Tonight, I am too sad to say we will make a wish on the new moon, as I normally do.

Who or what could we wish for? Rescue for ourselves, for Lord and Lady Milton, for Hart, for all the good kind people on board? For the woman who played the harmonica to her children to the last moment? For the brave men of the orchestra, who gave us comfort? For old Mr. and Mrs. Straus, who were never seen one without the other? Is she alone in a lifeboat without him?

The moon illuminates white patches covering the surface of the water. They might be giant seabirds, resting on outspread wings, waiting like us until morning. But they are not birds. They float, some with faces submerged, others turned towards the sky–bodies, held up by cork life jackets.

"Don't cry, Gardy," Miss Portia says.

Dawn arrives, and with it the palest of pink clouds amidst a glitter of color–green and violet and softest blue–shimmering and glistening on the tall white sails of ships that surround us. *Rescue at last!*

"Icebergs," the oarsmen cry hoarsely. *And I thought they were ships!* Now our small convoy of boats is in greater danger than ever before! A whistle shrills through the silence.

A voice calls out, "Get us off."

"Aye, aye, sir, Officer Lightoller," one of our crewmen answers hoarsely. He cuts us loose from the other boats and rows towards the capsized collapsible. We shift, trying to make room for survivors. As many as twenty or thirty are helped aboard.

One of the officers says, "This was the last of the four collapsibles to leave the *Titanic*. It capsized as it hit the surface. We are mostly crew and officers. We've been kneeling or standing for hours, knee-deep in water. One of my men is trapped beneath the boat–his legs are badly damaged, broken I'm afraid. We could not have lasted much longer. Thank God we sighted you!"

Our boat sinks lower in the water with the weight of the extra passengers. We were overloaded before, but now we are crammed together so close that some women must stand. No one complains.

A stoker is pulled aboard. His face is covered in soot, and his thin shirt is torn to shreds. He trembles so violently with cold, I hear his teeth chatter. Someone winds a muffler around his neck. A woman tears her blanket in half and folds up one part as a pillow for the man with broken legs. I take off my coat to cover one of the shivering sailors. Someone in another boat might do the same for Patrick.

Officer Lightoller is the last to jump into our boat. He points to the man with broken legs: "It is thanks to this chap, we are saved. Look there, coming towards us, braving the icebergs, is a ship answering his SOS. Remember this man's name, Harold Bride, our radio operator. He would not leave his post until Captain Smith ordered us to abandon ship! Hang on, man," Officer Lightoller says. "You'll soon be safe!"

We cheer. *A ship, coming to help us!*

Miss Portia whispers to me, her lips blue with cold, "I made a wish on the moon, Gardy, and it came true!"

Nothing has ever looked as beautiful to me–this ship, with only one black funnel; this ship, not even half as big as the *Titanic*, but braving the dangerous seas to rescue us. Another cheer goes up as the first of the lifeboats draws to the shelter of the ship's side. Ladders are lowered for the first boatload to climb aboard. Soon it will be our turn.

The wind has risen, and water begins to swell and ripple into waves strong enough to wash over the sides of our boat. We were full when we started out, but now, with our second load of survivors, we must number over seventy!

Officer Lightoller does his best to move our lifeboat closer to the ship, but we sit so low in the water that we make no progress at all. Every wave that advances us a few yards also pushes us out again. Each time, it seems, we are carried further away from safety. *Have we come so far only to perish now?*

We wait and hope. Watch canvas bags being lowered over the side for the children, eager hands lifting survivors onto the deck. It is light enough now for me to read the name painted on the ship's side. She is named *Carpathia*.

We are the last boat to come in, all of us too cold and wet to speak. My mind is numb, and I no longer hope nor despair. One great swell of water threatens to swamp our lifeboat, then, mercifully, heaves us close enough to reach the ladders and safety.

The children are helped into the canvas bags. Harry Bride, the wounded radio operator, is hoisted on board, looking pitifully white and still. After all that he has done and suffered, he will surely survive.

16

Carpathia

I t is my turn. Ropes are passed around my waist, and I climb halfway up the rungs of the ladder. I look down, stop, and realize I cannot go even one step more. Every bone and muscle in my body refuses to obey this final task. I lean my forehead against my arm and close my eyes. The children are safely on board; that is all that matters.

"You are almost here. Look up, girl, you can do it!" Of course I can, I have come this far. *Get a hold of yourself, Louisa Gardener. Others are waiting behind you.*

I raise my head to see a sailor's face smile encouragement from above. Painfully, I pull myself up the remaining rungs towards him. Strong arms lift me the last few feet, and the rope around my waist is removed. Someone wraps a dry blanket around my shoulders and I clutch it. I had forgotten what it feels like to be warm.

Miss Portia and Miss Alexandra greet me as if we had been parted for days! They cling to my legs. Lady Milton and Hart are here, too. Hart and I hug each other, forgetful of place. Lady Milton comes towards us, and Hart steps back, an arm around each of the girls. Lady Milton takes my cold hands in hers.

"Thank you, Gardener, for my daughters' lives." Her hands drop to her sides. "This was the last boat. My husband...was he, is he, in the boat with you?" she asks.

I wish with all my heart that I could reply differently. "No, ma'am. I am sorry, but we saw him only before we left."

"Mama, Mama, Papa gave me a letter to give to Roger. Don't cry, Mama, you can have it!" Miss Portia hands the damp boarding pass to her mother.

"Thank you, my darling. What a good girl you are to keep it safe. We will give it to Roger when we come home." She turns away. Her whispered "He has gone, Hart!" breaks my heart.

An officer hurries us downstairs, where we are given dry clothes and broth or coffee to drink. A steward tells Lady Milton a cabin has been made available for her and the children. The doctor will come to see her presently. Hart and I follow, carrying clothing donated by the *Carpathia*'s passengers. Everything possible seems to have been prepared for us.

I remove the children's damp things and hang them on hooks to dry. The girls fall asleep instantly, in the second bunk. A tap on the door and a steward informs us that a service of thanks is to be held in the main lounge for the *Titanic*'s survivors, followed by one of prayer for those who perished.

Lady Milton insists on attending. Hart goes with her, and I stay behind to watch over the children. I do not believe that our crowded lifeboat could have lasted much longer if the *Carpathia* had not arrived when she did. I sit and listen to the children breathe. Now and again, one of them sobs in her sleep.

I murmur, "We are all safe now," hoping it is true.

When Lady Milton returns, she can barely speak. "Captain Rostron says he has not found any survivors, other than the 705 he was able to rescue. He has circled the area several times where the *Titanic* sank. More than 1,500 people are gone. I am a widow, on a ship of widows." Lady Milton is white as a ghost and looks as if she is about to faint. She refuses to sit, though Hart offers her a chair.

"Please, Gardener, repeat every word my husband said to you," Lady Milton asks.

"Yes, ma'am. Miss Portia and I were about to climb down into the lifeboat behind Miss Alexandra when Miss Portia cried, 'Papa.' Somehow, Lord Milton must have persuaded the officer to let him through to find us. He grasped Miss Portia's hand for an instant, gave her the boarding pass for safekeeping, and told me to look after the children, your ladyship. 'I promised my wife,' he said. Then he disappeared back into the crowd."

Miss Portia sits up in the bunk. "Papa said, 'God bless you both, my darlings' and asked me to give the card to Roger. Will Papa come back soon?"

Lady Milton goes to her daughter, touches her cheek, and crumples down beside the sleeping Miss Alexandra. I tiptoe out of the cabin.

The corridors are full of passengers looking for family members and friends. I scan their faces, hoping to see a familiar one. Suddenly I am confronted by Roberts, holding the baby boy in her arms. I almost believe she has come looking for me!

At that moment, Hart appears. "Well, I never, if it isn't Roberts. So you made it safely. But where is your other little charge?"

"I am going to make a new life in Canada, and I'm asking you two to hold your tongues. I was not able to save Loraine. Her parents would not let her leave without them. Before I could persuade them, an officer bundled me into a boat with Trevor. They stayed behind.

"I'm leaving England for good! I never took anything that was not rightly mine to take, and you can't prove otherwise. I'll thank you to keep out of my way and to mind your own business." She pushes past us, leaving us both too shocked to speak for several minutes.

Eventually Hart says, "We'll never find the truth out about that one, or what really happened at the end on the *Titanic*. The baby's relatives will undoubtedly take care of him when the *Carpathia* reaches New York. There is nothing we can do, Gardener. At least Miss Loraine was with her parents at the end!" Hart straightens her shoulders, as if determined to banish any more sad thoughts.

"And now, we had better find out where everything is. It will be time for lunch soon—goodness knows how and where they'll feed us all! Her ladyship needs every bit of her strength. She has the new baby to consider now!"

All I can think of is that poor little girl and her family and if Roberts spoke the truth. There are so many missing from the *Titanic*. *What happened to Tim, the glass-washer? Does he have a mother or wife waiting for him?* Mrs. Landers is safe—I saw her earlier. *But did Patrick escape the boiler room?*

"You look as if you have seen a ghost," Hart says, biting her lip. "I'm sorry, Gardener. Won't we all be seeing ghosts after this!"

After supper, Hart and I go in search of a place to sleep. Many of those on the *Carpathia* have given up their cabins, but passengers from both ships lie on tables, on the floor of the public rooms, on mattresses, or on deck chairs. Women passengers are cutting down skirts, coats, and blankets to clothe some of the children and those with nothing to wear.

Hart and I are given two blankets each and find a corner of the lounge to lie down. Neither of us can settle—there is so much we have not had time to talk about. I prop myself on my elbow, trying to get comfortable on the floor. I'm not ready to close my eyes yet. "Where were you, Hart? We looked and looked for you on deck."

"I went back to the cabin to get my life jacket, and you'd gone. Then we went up to search for you. The officer on the port side told Lord and Lady Milton that all first-class ladies, children, and maids were to go down to A deck, that lifeboat 4 was being lowered there for us. It would be a shorter distance to climb into from the A deck windows. Captain's orders, he said. Lady Milton told the officer to send you down to us and described you. Well, nothing went the way it was supposed to after that!

"We found the windows were locked, and a sailor had to be sent to look for the key. Then the officer discovered a sounding bar, which measures the depth of the water, sticking out beneath the lifeboat. It had to be chopped away. While we waited, the officer went up to the boat deck to help lower other boats.

"Lady Milton was frantic about the children. I tried to get back up to look for you and was sent down. Finally Lord Milton insisted he be permitted to look for his daughters! When he returned, he said he had seen all three of you climb safely into a lifeboat, and that calmed her ladyship. It was hours before the sounding bar was chopped away and the windows unlocked. We were helped through. Deck chairs were placed end to end, like steps, for us to clamber down into the boat. It was women and children only. Two boys would have been turned away, with the other men, but their fathers swore they had not yet turned thirteen.

"Lady Milton refused to leave without her husband! He begged her to think of Master Roger and the girls and the new baby. He promised that he and Colonel Astor would assist each other. And so I helped Lady Milton down into the lifeboat.

"I feel sorry for young Lady Astor—all she has left of the colonel are the gloves he threw to her before we set off. She was very brave. Do you know she expects her first child in a few weeks?

"And we had waited so long that we were one of the last boats to leave the ship!" Hart's cheeks are flushed with indignation. And the worst of it is, there would have been room for some of the gentlemen! I hear Lord and Lady Duff Gordon, who left in one of the earliest boats, were two of only twelve passengers and crew–all those seats left empty! There will not be many ladies ordering new gowns from *Madame Lucile's!* Yes, that's who Lady Duff Gordon is–the owner of *Madame Lucile's*–and to think Lady Milton orders some of her gowns from her salon! I heard someone say that her husband persuaded the crew not to row back for survivors, he was so afraid of being swamped! Wicked and selfish, I call it."

"It may not be true, Hart. When I first came on deck with the girls, many of the ladies refused to enter the lifeboats, thinking it was safer to stay on board. At first, I thought the same thing. And I am sure I saw Lady Milton speaking to that lady this evening," I say.

"That's because her ladyship will not turn her back on a friend," Hart says. "But I'll tell you one thing, Gardener: Someone will have to answer for what happened on the *Titanic*. All those families left without fathers, husbands, sons, and daughters...babies drowned! I'll never forget the cries of those people sliding or jumping from the deck, disappearing like ants down a hole." Hart blinks away tears.

"I know. Later that night, when I came out of the gymnasium where I had taken the children to warm up, I saw that only a few boats remained. Men were held back by the crew, and there were long lines of women and children. You could see that not everyone would get a place on the lifeboats, Hart. I kept thinking, over and over, *don't let it happen again, don't let me lose another one!* I had to make sure the girls were safe. Why build a fine boat like the *Titanic* and not make room for enough lifeboats?" I ask her.

"That's no big secret, Gardener. The White Star Line wanted more room for first-class passengers to promenade. It's always been like that—the rich come first!"

Hart stretches out her hand to me. "Tell me, Louisa...well, that's your name, isn't it? What did you mean by another one?"

I take her hand. We are friends now. "When I was four, maybe five, Mother told my sister Kathleen and me that we were to watch over our little brother. It was our first time to play at the seaside. I made shell patterns in the sand. Kath and I forgot about Johnny...he slipped away and drowned. I've been frightened of the terrible power of the ocean, of water, ever since!"

"Do you know what you are, Louisa Gardener? A real heroine, that's what, and I am proud to be your friend. Now go to sleep, it's over." But it isn't over....

The storm begins in the early hours of the morning and rages on and on. Thunder, lightning, wind, and fog. We can scarcely keep our balance. Each time the foghorn blows her warning dirge, I think of those who are not with us anymore.

At roll call, we listen, horrified, to the absence of name after name. *Will Mother and Father believe I have drowned, too?* And Kathleen's Patrick–I shall have to tell her!

Hart says, "Lady Milton has cabled home and asked Mr. Briggs to let your family know you are safe."

For the remainder of the voyage, the weather is too fierce for us to go out on deck. I am at my wit's end keeping Miss Portia and Miss Alexandra occupied. The worst has happened and may happen again, but my fears are buried at the bottom of the sea. Only a great sadness remains to haunt me.

On Wednesday morning, April 18th, the *Carpathia* sails into New York harbor. In spite of the cold and rain, passengers gather on deck in their borrowed clothes, anxious to be on dry land once again.

Crowds, hushed, under their umbrellas, are gathered to greet us as we step onto the gangway. The family is immediately ushered into a waiting area, where friends and relatives wait for news. Lady Milton falls into her sister's arms, whose husband, Lord Fenton, bends down to embrace the girls.

"Where is Papa?" Miss Alexandra asks.

Lord and Lady Fenton lead us away from the cries of joy and despair all around us and into a waiting automobile. Hart nudges my elbow, pointing to where Roberts, holding baby Trevor, is posing for newspaper photographers. No doubt she has told them how she "saved" the baby. Loraine's name and those of her parents are not on the list of survivors.

Three days after we reach New York, Lord Milton's body and that of Colonel Astor are found by the *Mackay-Bennett*. The ship was sent out from Halifax, Nova Scotia, Canada, to recover bodies from the *Titanic*.

Early in May, we sail home on the *Adriatic*. Hart says she thought she glimpsed Mr. Ismay, managing director of the White Star Line, come on board. If she did, we never saw him. He must have stayed in his cabin for the entire voyage. Ashamed to face us, no doubt! His manservant was not on the list of survivors....

London, England

1912

17

Home

It is good to be back again at Chesham Place, even under such sad circumstances. Mrs. Ransom distributes black armbands, as Lady Milton does not wish the staff to be in full mourning.

Hart and I are given new uniforms, sewn by Mrs. Wilson. Lady Fenton has provided us with day and afternoon wear, bought ready-made from one of New York's department stores. Mrs. Wilson does not approve of them. "They'll not last a month!" she says.

Mr. Briggs hands us envelopes, in addition to our month's wages. "Lady Milton wishes you to replace any personal items lost in the sinking," he says. It is kind of her to think of us in her grief. I find five new one-pound notes in mine, which amounts to six months' extra wages. I'll give Kathleen two pounds to replace her spring coat, an extra pound for Mother, and save the rest.

I have been given Saturday afternoon to go home. Mrs. Ransom says that I may return half an hour later than usual. It's hard to wait even one more day to see my family again! I warn Miss Portia and Miss Alexandra ahead of time. They are afraid to let me out of their sight since the disaster. I explain that I have not seen my parents and brothers and sisters for almost a month.

"I promise I will look in on you when I come home, but you must promise to be good girls and go straight to sleep," I tell them.

Nanny Mackintosh is quick to interrupt me: "Since when does one give explanations to children of one's presence or absence, Gardener? Is this some new method of child-rearing that you have acquired in America?"

"No, Nanny Mackintosh." I can see by her expression that I am to be put in my place once and for all.

It began with a battle over the night-light. We arrived home late yesterday, sad and tired from our journey. Miss Portia continues to have nightmares, but I have found a night-light to comfort her. I dared to suggest to Nanny that the child be allowed this for a while longer.

"Indeed, Gardener? In my experience, I have yet to meet a nursemaid capable of making useful suggestions, let alone decisions!"

"I beg your pardon, Nanny Mackintosh, I thought—"

"You are not paid to think, Gardener, but to obey my instructions! Giving in to Miss Portia's fears solves nothing. It is obvious that the girls have been thoroughly indulged! The sinking of the *Titanic* and the sad loss of their father must not be made an excuse to give in to their every whim."

How can she be so hard? It is not so long ago that she lost her own father. Nanny no longer frightens me with her scolding.

"Nanny Mackintosh, I would be very much obliged if you would permit a night-light, at least until after Lord Milton's funeral. In New York, both Lady Milton and Lady Fenton gave their approval for Miss Portia to have one." I wait for another of Nanny's homilies, but to my surprise she concedes.

"Very well, Gardener, a few days more!"

The next day, she is occupied with making a list of requirements to replenish the children's wardrobe. She shares Mrs. Wilson's opinion of the clothes Lady Fenton has bought them. She decides to send me to the park with the children without her this afternoon.

"I trust you will refrain from discussing any private matters pertaining to the family, Gardener," Nanny says.

It is a relief to leave both Nanny and the house on such a warm and beautiful spring day. Hart had warned me that I'd find it hard to return to being just an extra pair of hands for Nanny. I did not anticipate how much I would object to her constant disapproval. *Was she this critical before our departure? Or have I changed?* If it were not for my great affection for the children, my respect for Lady Milton, and Hart's friendship, I might think about seeking employment elsewhere. But I suspect that other nurseries would not be so very different. Nanny Gilbert says she discharged her new nursemaid for insolence. Poor thing, she probably had the temerity to venture an opinion!

I reply briefly and politely to the nannies' questions about the *Titanic*, and we leave the park earlier than usual. I am uneasy and suspect we are being watched. The newspapers do occasionally write of child kidnappings!

There are footsteps behind us. I look over my shoulder. *Is that man following us?* I can't be sure, but I hurry the girls along, frightened now. There isn't a constable in sight. I pick up Miss Alexandra, and we run the rest of the way home.

All three of us are hot and breathless when we get to the back door. I close it behind us and wipe the children's faces and my own with cool water at the scullery sink, before going into the kitchen.

Mrs. Porter looks at my flushed face and invites us to sit down and rest before we go upstairs. "Croft, fetch three glasses and a pitcher of lemonade from the larder, please. Hot, isn't it, Gardener?" She offers a ladyfinger biscuit to the girls.

They beam at her, as if she had presented some precious gift. They consider sitting down at Mrs. Porter's kitchen table to be a great treat. Miss Alexandra drinks the entire glass of lemonade without spilling a drop.

Miss Portia asks, "Is it a party? I wish our papa was coming too!" Croft turns away, and it is all I can do not to cry. Before we can pull ourselves together, there is a loud knock at the back door.

Croft answers it and returns quickly. "Please, Mrs. Porter, it's a gentleman from the *Daily Sketch* newspaper. He wants to talk to Gardener about the *Titanic* and to take a photograph of the children. What am I to tell him?"

"Nothing, Croft, I'll deal with him," Mrs. Porter says, looking grim.

"A man followed us here from the park, Mrs. Porter," I whisper.

She rolls down her sleeves, smoothes her apron,

and picks up her rolling pin. Her voice carries, and we manage to hear every word.

"You are to leave the girl alone. Lady Milton does not permit interviews! Photograph? I have never heard of such impertinence. How dare you intrude at such a time! Be off, before I call the constable and have you arrested. You are trespassing! No hawkers or circulars!" The outside door slams shut.

Mrs. Porter marches back into the kitchen, rolling down her cuffs. "If he shows his face here again, he'll feel the weight of my rolling pin!" she says indignantly.

"Please, Mrs. Porter, may Alexandra and I feel the rolling pin, too?" Miss Portia asks. Croft puts her hand over her mouth, and her shoulders shake. I burst out laughing, and Mrs. Porter joins in. The door opens, and Nanny Mackintosh appears, looking as if she is about to have apoplexy.

"Is there something you require, Nanny Mackintosh?" Mrs. Porter asks. "It will soon be time to bring up your tea—there's a nice jam sponge cooling in the larder."

Nanny Mackintosh ignores her, turning her wrath on me. "Have you completely taken leave of your senses, Gardener? Take the girls upstairs immediately and change them for tea!"

"Thank you very much for the lemonade, Mrs. Porter. Come along, Miss Portia, Miss Alexandra." I walk out wishing that Nanny Mackintosh might get a taste of Mrs. Porter's rolling pin! Upstairs, I settle the girls in the bedroom with their dolls and wait.

Nanny storms in. "Explain yourself, Gardener." If she brings out the castor oil, I'll refuse to take it. "Don't keep me waiting," she says ominously.

"We were hot, Nanny Mackintosh. Mrs. Porter kindly offered us lemonade. It was a treat for the children."

"Eating with servants, in the kitchen, is never a treat, Gardener–it confuses the children. There must be a line that they may not cross. Kitchen gossip is not fit conversation for Lady Milton's daughters to listen to!"

"But, Nanny, we are servants too. We eat with the children at every meal, and they are in my company all day long."

"You are either stupid or deliberately impertinent! I shall have to discuss the matter with Mrs. Ransom. She will make the decision whether to trouble Lady Milton at this difficult time. I have made excuses for your inexperience for too long!"

I make no reply. Thank goodness tomorrow is Saturday and I can go home!

Mother and Emmy are waiting for me at the door. The twins grin bashfully, and little George pulls at my skirt, wanting to be picked up. When we have gone inside and the kissing and hugging and a few joyful tears are over, Father turns to me.

"Well, now, it's good to have you home, Lou. Your mother has been baking ever since she heard you were back safe and sound!" The entire kitchen table is covered with cakes, scones, biscuits, and pies. It looks like a coronation tea!

I have to describe the sinking and the rescue, the wait in the lifeboats, and the climb up the ladder to the *Carpathia*. I leave out some things, but manage to tell how beautiful and elegant the ship was! And when I am all talked out, I ask Father how it is that he is home early from the market on a Saturday afternoon.

"Isn't this your busiest time, Father?"

"Nothing that can't wait for my Lou's return," he says, and that almost makes me cry again. He pats my hand, suddenly shy at showing any emotion. Then he lifts Emily onto his knee.

"Your uncle Alf and I have taken on an assistant. Do you remember young Patrick O'Connor, Lou?" Father says.

"Patrick, you don't mean Kathleen's Patrick? I thought he had drowned. His name was not on the list of survivors, Father."

"He never went!" my father says.

"Who's talking about Patrick? Lou, oh, Lou, you're home!" Kathleen rushes in and throws her arms around my neck. I am so thankful that I will not have to tell Kathleen that her Patrick is at the bottom of the ocean with the *Titanic*. Mother dabs her eyes again–her apron must be quite damp by now!

"Oh, Lou, when I think of you and those little girls and..." Mother says.

"If you start crying again, Harry and me are going out to play. Can we please, Mother?" my little brother Tom asks, itching to get away.

"There's sausages for supper; don't be late," Mother says.

Tom hurries out after Harry, turns at the door, runs back, and tweaks my hair. "We told Mother you'd never drown!" he says and disappears.

"Now, Flo," Father says, "she's home safe and sound and none the worse! Sit down and drink your tea. As for Patrick, Lou, I reckon he's had a lucky escape, though he did not think so at the time. He was one of a group of stokers who'd missed the early train from London, or so he told us!" Father gives Kathleen a stern look. "Not that it is any of my business." Kathleen suppresses a smile.

"When they arrived at the ship, he said the crew's gangway was just being pulled up. They were told their positions had been given to replacements–men who'd been waiting for hours, hoping to get taken on. Well, next day, Patrick turns up at the market. He offers to put in two days work, for no pay, to show us what he can do. I tell you, that lad is never idle for a minute. Truth is, I don't know how Alf and I ever managed without him!" Father goes out for a smoke.

Mother looks pleased. "Take your sister upstairs, Kathleen. You must have a lot to talk about. Emmy can lend me a hand getting supper. She's a real help now. She made those scones all by herself. Do you want fried bread with your sausages, Lou?"

"Please, Mother. Come here, Emmy, and let me take a look at you. You haven't said a word. My goodness, you're growing tall! I don't know where my little sister went. I can see who will be baking all the fancy cakes for Kathleen's salon one of these days!"

Upstairs, in the room we shared for so long, Kathleen tells me that Patrick has been asked twice for Sunday tea.

"Father says he sees no reason why we can't walk out, seeing as I've turned sixteen." Love found Kath early. I would not be a bit surprised if one day they became engaged! Mother and Father seem to have taken a real liking to Patrick.

At first, Kathleen won't hear of taking any money for a new coat.

"You have no idea what that coat meant to me, Kathleen. I felt so proud wearing it on deck in the moonlight, just as you said I should. It kept the girls and me from freezing in the lifeboat. It covered a half-drowned sailor, and now it has been cut down for two little children who were rescued wearing only their nightclothes." I insist she take the money to buy another coat.

Father walks all the way back to Chesham Place with me–he has never done such a thing before. "We are that proud of you and grateful you were spared!" he tells me.

Two days after Lord Milton's funeral–after Master Roger had been driven back to school, pale and refusing to shed a tear in front of us–Nanny and I are asked to bring the girls down to say good-bye to their grandmother. Lady Portman will be returning home early tomorrow morning. Miss Alexandra is out of sorts, bewildered by the many comings and goings in the house. She cries and does not want to say good-bye.

"With your permission, Lady Milton, Lady Portman, Miss Alexandra is overtired and should be put to bed," Nanny says. Lady Milton agrees, her thoughts elsewhere, I think.

"Gardener, take Miss Alexandra upstairs immediately, please," Nanny says.

"No! Don't want to!" The child rubs her eyes with her fists.

"Come along, I will read you a nice story when you

are in bed," I coax her, and she takes my hand. I hear
Nanny sigh her disapproval. *What's wrong now?*

"Will you read to me, too, Gardy, when I am in
bed?" Miss Portia asks.

Nanny Mackintosh, her face mottled with anger,
answers before I have a chance to reply: "Must I
remind you again, Miss Portia, that big girls of five
are old enough to remember that pet names are not
permitted in my nursery. There will be no more stories until you ask Gardener correctly."

Lady Milton rises from the sofa. Her face is pale
and stern.

"You have said quite enough, Nanny Mackintosh.
You will not bully either my daughters or Gardener
in this way. What does it matter what the children
call the person who saved their lives? It is a pity that
you are not as fond of children as she is. Girls, you
may go upstairs now with..." Lady Milton hesitates,
"...with Gardy. She will read to you both. Mama is
tired."

"I beg your pardon, Lady Milton." Nanny Mackintosh
sails out the room. *Gardy?*

Miss Portia runs to her mother and puts her arms
around her neck, then kisses both her mother and
grandmother. As I close the drawing-room door
behind us, I hear Lady Milton's brokenhearted words,
"Mother, how can we manage without him?"

Upstairs, there is no sign of Nanny. No doubt she

is complaining to Mrs. Ransom! I do not see Nanny again that night, but she presides over breakfast and lunch as usual. No word is said about the incident and no comment made when Miss Portia does not finish everything on her plate.

18

Changes

Next day, when we return from our afternoon walk, Nanny's door is ajar, the room is bare, and the bed has been stripped. Hart passes me in the corridor as we come in and whispers, "Nanny Mackintosh has left for good!" She must have spent the afternoon packing her things. Hart is called away, so I don't have a chance to hear any more before we go upstairs.

Phipps brings up our tea tray and sets out cups and plates for three. "Tea, for my three beautiful ladies," he says. Miss Portia and Miss Alexandra bat their eyelashes at him, but I take no notice. So it must be true—Nanny Mackintosh really has gone. Phipps would never have been so impertinent if she'd been here! And I would have been blamed for sure by Nanny...accused of encouraging him. Sometimes I wonder if Mr. Phipps is suited to being a footman. But I admit I enjoy his teasing, now that I've become used to it.

The children settle to playing with their dollhouse after tea, and I clear the table before ringing the bell. Dean comes up to collect the tray.

"Lady Milton wants to see you in the drawing room. I'm to stay with the girls until you return."

I change my apron and cap, feeling as nervous as I did a year ago, when I was first interviewed. I wonder what she wants. The only thing I can think of is that I am going to be dismissed. *Then who will look after Miss Portia and Miss Alexandra if both Nanny and I are gone?*

Before she left, I am sure Nanny Mackintosh complained about me to Mrs. Ransom. Nanny had warned me that she would do so. And it is Mrs. Ransom who advises Lady Milton about staff changes.

As Mother said, girls are always ready to jump at the chance of working in a good place. It will break my heart to leave, but I am not sorry for disagreeing with Nanny Mackintosh. Rigid, that's what she was, unkind and unbending. Miss Portia and Miss Alexandra need a bit of extra love and attention just now. I straighten my cap and knock at the drawing-room door.

"Thank you, Hart, you may leave us now. I will ring when Gardener and I have finished our talk." Hart leaves, without so much as a glance at me. That's not a good sign. I notice Lady Milton's untouched tea tray. Hart said she's not eating enough for one, let alone two!

"I will come straight to the point, Gardener. Nanny Mackintosh has decided to return to Edinburgh permanently, to be closer to her widowed mother. This leaves my daughters without a nanny. May I be frank with you, Gardener?"

Whatever Lady Milton has in mind, I know it will turn out to be something unpleasant! That's what being frank usually means.

"You are still very young and, over the last few weeks, you have had to shoulder a great deal of responsibility. More than one would expect of someone twice your age..."

Lady Milton does not sound as if she is going to dismiss me without a character. She is only saying that I am too young and inexperienced.

"I have discussed the matter with my mother, and we are in complete agreement. I would like you to stay on as nanny. The children and I would not want to be without you!" *I am to be kept on? I am not to be dismissed, after all?* I can hardly believe it, I was so sure...

"Please think carefully before you answer, Gardener. Do you feel that you are able to continue to be in charge of Miss Portia and my naughty little Alexandra? We have spoiled her, I am afraid. Her papa doted on her."

"Miss Alexandra wants to be independent. She is a sweet good girl. I am quite firm with her, ma'am. I would like to stay very much, Lady Milton."

"I am so pleased to hear that, Gardener. We hoped you would. You, Hart, the girls, and I have been through more together than anyone can ever comprehend! I hope you will remain as nanny and as friend and companion to my daughters for many years. I am sure this is what my husband would have wished too. He told me you would look after them, after he saw you."

"Oh, ma'am..." My eyes fill with tears. It isn't fair, the children fatherless!

"I will expect you to bring any nursery problems to me. I must try to be both mother and father to my children now." Lady Milton also seems close to tears, but composes herself and continues calmly. "Now for practical matters...I will inform Mrs. Ransom what has been decided. Your salary will be raised immediately to sixteen pounds a year and to twenty pounds in a year's time. We will spend the summer with Lady Portman. Master Roger will join us there. My mother will return home with us and stay until after the baby's arrival. A baby nurse will be hired for the early months. Good can take over nursery cleaning duties. Do you find her capable?"

"Yes, ma'am. She is a nice, hardworking girl. Her windows are perfect!"

"I can see that the nursery is going to be a much happier place from now on. Thank you, Gardener. I will be up later to say good night to the children."

I pass by Hart in the hall. She says, "I was wrong, wasn't I? Things are changing, and about time too!" She must have known.

I take the nursery stairs two at a time, then, remembering my new position, slow down. *Why? Who is going to tell me what to do, or how to behave?* I can run or walk as I please. I hurry on up, anxious to tell the girls that, from now on, I will be their nanny!

That night, when I go down for my cocoa and biscuits, the servants' hall is hushed. Everyone is gathered around the long table in complete silence. *Has something happened?* Mr. Briggs gets up and pulls out my chair for me.

"Good evening, Nanny," he says respectfully. I flush scarlet and look over my shoulder, half-expecting to see Nanny Mackintosh standing behind me. Croft comes in from the larder holding a large, white, iced cake, decorated with pink roses. Written in pink letters are the words WELCOME HOME, HART AND NANNY GARDENER.

"What a beautiful cake! Thank you, Mrs. Porter," Hart says. I am quite overwhelmed and can manage only a smile. Everyone applauds.

As usual, Phipps is the first to speak. "Is it to look at or to eat, Mrs. Porter?"

"That's for Hart and Nanny Gardener to say, seeing as I baked it for them!"

"It looks too nice to eat, Mrs. Porter, but it would be a shame to let it get stale, wouldn't it?" Hart replies. Mrs. Porter cuts everyone a generous slice and says she'll send up some for the children's tea next day, subject to my approval!

This time, I do find my voice. "You are kind, Mrs. Porter, thank you. The girls will love a treat. I'd better get back to the nursery so that Good can come down and enjoy a piece, too. And, Mrs. Porter, *you* know best about what to send up for nursery meals. Thank you again. Good night, all."

The children do not talk about what happened on the *Titanic*. But I watch and listen carefully, ready to answer their questions if need be. They have gradually come to accept that their papa will not be coming home.

On the last night of our stay in Amersham, I slip into the garden. It is a beautiful warm night, bright with stars and a new moon. This time, unafraid that Nanny will pounce when I return upstairs, I sit for a while on the swing, grateful for a slight breeze, listening to sounds of the garden.

A white-gowned figure tiptoes down the path towards me. She looks like a small ghost in her white nightgown, long fair hair, and bare feet.

"Miss Portia, whatever are you doing? Come here." I pull the little girl up beside me and put my arm round her. "Did you have a bad dream?" I ask.

She looks up at me. "What happened to the dogs and to Jenny's new kittens?" Here in the light of the new moon, the moon which can still bring back memories of other sorrows, I hope I can find the right answer.

"I am not sure, but I like to think of them in heaven with your papa, safe and happy. It's late— one last swing, and then we'll wave good-bye to the garden until next summer."

Hand in hand, we return to the house, tiptoe through the scullery and kitchen, through the green baize door, and upstairs to bed. "Shall I leave your window open a little, so you can see the moon?" I ask. But Miss Portia falls asleep instantly.

Baby Fiona is born the first week in September. Nanny Barnes has moved into Nanny Mackintosh's old room. She is full of stories about all the babies she has taken care of. She sings to Miss Fiona and encourages the girls to sit in the rocking chair and hold their baby sister. Born at such a sad time, Miss Fiona is the most contented of babies and in danger of being completely spoiled by an adoring household! Even Master Roger approves of his new sister. Nanny Barnes leaves us to look after another baby when Miss Fiona is a year old, and she settles into the nursery under my charge.

There are more changes. Lady Milton no longer entertains as much as she did when Lord Milton was alive. She has decided to manage with a smaller staff.

Phipps joins the army, which he has wanted to do for some time. Before he leaves, he asks if he may write to me and if I will write back! I tell him I will think it over, but I fully intend to reply. Mrs. Ransom accepts a position in a bigger establishment, and Mrs. Porter becomes cook/housekeeper. She and Mr. Briggs are strict, but fair.

Mr. Harris and Hart are officially keeping company, and we expect a wedding announcement any day. Hart told me that Mrs. Porter and Mr. Briggs had discussed the matter and said there would be no objection to her and Mr. Harris remaining in Lady Milton's service after their marriage!

Patrick and Kathleen announce their engagement and will marry when she turns eighteen. Emmy and I are to be bridesmaids, and Kathleen has already started to design the most splendid hats for the occasion. I hope Charlie will get leave so he can attend the wedding with me.

Mr. Briggs continues to read us bits from the *Times* newspaper, shaking his head and predicting a war. Just like Father, he mistrusts change. He still refers to me as Nanny Gardener, though everyone else, both upstairs and downstairs, calls me Gardy.

Afterword

The Gardener family, their friends, neighbors, and the staff and family of Lord and Lady Milton are imaginary. However, they exist in a real world with the public figures of the time and experience the life-changing events that occurred between 1911 and 1912. At the conclusion of the story in 1913, the First World War is only months away.

The passengers and crew on board the *Titanic* and the *Carpathia*, with the exception of Mrs. Landers, Tim, and Roberts (who are drawn from composite figures), are historically accurate. They lived or died on the ill-fated voyage.

The *Titanic* was heralded as the largest, most luxurious, and safest ocean liner ever constructed and yet

- 1,503 passengers and crew lost their lives, and only 705 people were saved.

- Even in death, social hierarchies were rigidly observed. The bodies of first-class passengers found at sea were placed in coffins on board the recovery ships sent out from Halifax, Nova Scotia, Canada. Second- and third-class passengers were placed in canvas bags. Steerage and crew were placed on ice in the ship's bow.

- Passengers who lived or died were remembered by name. Maids, nannies, and manservants were listed in the following way: Astor, Colonel J.J. and Manservant.

- Harold Bride, the radio operator, recovered in hospital from his ordeal.

- Within days and weeks of the tragedy, new seagoing regulations were put in place, the most significant being that sufficient lifeboat spaces must be provided for every person on board. Lifeboat drill and training for ship's crew became mandatory. Lifeboats were to be equipped with compasses and sufficient provisions. A twenty-four-hour watch was made compulsory on all ships.

- In 1913, an international ice patrol was established in North Atlantic waters to track icebergs during the spring and winter months.